SUMMER OF LOVE IN ALABAMA, SUMMER OF '06

BUNNY LAWNA D'JUELZ

Copyright © 2022 Bunny Lawna D'Juelz

Paperback: 978-1-63767-693-6
eBook: 978-1-63767-694-3
Library of Congress Control Number: 2022900900

All rights reserved. No part of this publication may be reproduced, distributed, or transmitted in any form or by any electronic or mechanical means, without the prior written permission of the publisher, except in the case of brief quotations embodied in critical reviews and certain other noncommercial uses permitted by copyright law.

This is a work of fiction

Ordering Information:

BookTrail Agency
8838 Sleepy Hollow Rd.
Kansas City, MO 64114

Printed in the United States of America

"In loving memory of Rahshai Stevenson"

Table of Contents

CHAPTER 1 1

CHAPTER 2 7
Dale County Alabama (late 2005)

CHAPTER 3 14
I Need a Babysitter

CHAPTER 4 17
I Can Feel a Layoff Coming

CHAPTER 5 19
Sniffing Out Each Other

CHAPTER 6 21
The Scare While Taking Khalid to Work

CHAPTER 7 23
"Journey Meets the music producer"

CHAPTER 8 25
"I Can Feel a Layoffs in Dale County"

CHAPTER 9 27
"Journey & Khalid Meet Again"

CHAPTER 10 29
"Hired to Work at MRO Houston County"

CHAPTER 11 31
"Applying For That Apartment"

CHAPTER 12 34
"Journey & Ishmael Stay with the Music Producer & his family"

Chapter 13 36
"Journey Remembers That She Had Applied for An Apartment"

Chapter 14 38
"Okaloosa County"

Chapter 15 40
"The Car Repossession Department"

Chapter 16 42
"Brought Down to Your Level: Now I See You"

Chapter 17 47
"The Co-Sign for An Automobile"

Chapter 18 49
"The Meet Up in Houston County with Khalid's Affiliates"

Chapter 19 51
"Khalid goes to Work, Journey crosses state lines to cheat"

Chapter 20 56
"The Drop-Off & Late-Night Phone Call"

Chapter 21 59
"Crossing State Lines for Work"

Chapter 22 61
"Keys to My Place"

Chapter 23 63
"I Rebuke You in the Name of Jesus"

Chapter 24 66
"Journey & Khalid Fight"

Chapter 25 67
"Flex Returns"

Chapter 26 69
"A Night of Conversations Spent at Khalid's Mom's House"

Chapter 27 71
"They Make Love"

Chapter 28 72
"It's Your Birthday; I Wanna Show You What I Do"

Chapter 29 75
"The Decision to Change"

Chapter 30 77
"To Escambia County for rehab"

Chapter 31 79
"Lauren Talks with Journey"

Chapter 32 80
"Journey and Ishmael Visit & Support Khalid While He Goes Through Rehab"

Chapter 33 83
"In the Night Journey Dreams About Khalid"

Chapter 34 85
"Journey & Flex Fall Out Via Cell Phone"

Chapter 35 87
"Don't Act As if You Don't See Him"

Chapter 36 89
"Sex By the Seaside"

Chapter 37 91
"Journey Visits Khalid at Another Rehab"

Chapter 38 95
"Journey Tells Khalid 'Bye' "

Chapter 39 96
"Journey Goes to Be with Her Cousin in Clarksville, Kentucky"

Chapter 40 98
"Khalid's Death"

Chapter 41 100
"While Being in New Jersey"

Chapter 42 104
"I Miss You"

Chapter 43 106
"I Will Always Love You"

Chapter 1

It was an event filled day for Journey. She was just walking into her huge house that felt like home. Apart from all the other chaos and the worries of the world. It was her usual day to be consumed into her business dealings so, there was the constant ringing of her cell phone. Yet Journey had another idea about how she planned to spend her day. Taking her usual high volumes of phone calls were not inclusive.

She decided today to be very limited on the phone calls that she would take, coming in from her business world. She practically decided not to answer her phone calls at all. It was a Friday morning, and in her mind from her latest custom, Preparation Day. Time for her to take some time out to prepare for Saturday, in which she honored as Sabbath Day, she wished to prepare for it.

The phone rang just as she entered the door of her very large home, with very large front doors. She rushed in through her large doors in enough time to hear the phones ringing and to view the caller I.d. in order to make good decision as to whether to answer it or not. She saw the I.d. but she didn't fully recognize the caller. So she thought to herself, 'just this one call'. The name seemed familiar.

She had in mind prior to walking through her front door to get as couple as she could get. She would let nothing to get in her way as she dressed down a bit to make herself as comfortable as she would like to be. She would not like to let anything to slow her down from doing just that. Not even a phone call. While taking this phone call and while speaking on the phone. She began to pace around. As soon as she recognized the voice on the other end of the phone, Journey was filled with excitement. She recognized the caller's voice.

Meantime, preoccupied with the call and all, she quickly unwrapped the scarf from around her neck wishing to gain a bit more comfort. When Journey rushed through the door to answer the phone, Khalid, who was preoccupied in his thoughts upstairs in the upstairs office suite, heard noise in the house.

He was decked out in a nice white suit, baby blue shirt and a nice swirly blue & silver colored tie, his feet embellished by nice looking dress shoes. Since he heard the noise coming from the downstairs of the home, the noise of the door opening to be exact. He wanted to be assured that it was someone who belonged in the house, that had made entry way, and not some unauthorized visitor or a mischief stumbling into the neighborhood and through the house door.

"Mom is that you?", her son Khalid yelled out as he trotted down the stairs. Khalid had a nice thin, athletic sculpted body. He could hear his mother capture the phone. He could tell by the time that he had made it to the bottom of the stairs that she had gotten enraptured up into the phone call. He heard the pleasantness in her voice and the enthusiasm in her face over the short conversation. He took a pause prior to reaching the bottom of the staircase. He wanted to admire his mother. He always enjoyed watching his mother at work. He looked up to her work ethic. It caused a lot of troubles for them when he was in his youth, but he found no fault in her ethics. In his mind, she was the best momma. He continued down the stairs with a warm greeting smile.

Khalid rushed over to her to help Journey with her jacket & he grabbed hold of her scarf to lighten her load. For the time being he put things away for her into where they belonged. Which just so happened to be on the coat rack near the closet nearest to the house entry door. As he began to put her things away, the jacket, her scarf, her stylish hat even her gloves, her husband William had come out of the kitchen just as Khalid was tending to Journey's things.

As Journey was still pacing and making her best attempts to keep the phone conversation short with her old friend, He was yelling back and forth to Davis who happened to be in the kitchen with him helping with preparing the cater order for the day. Davis as a favor became help for him. He operated as an assistant chef within Williams' small kitchen team.

He took notice to Journey as he was in mid-conversation of yelling instructions back to Davis for the kitchen team, the team were busy as bees. Khalid wondered if there was any buzzing. He briefly visited into the kitchen to grab his mother and himself some snacks.

Journey too happened to be mid-conversation when William puckered up his lips to Journey just as she entered a greeting to whomever it was that she happened to be on the phone with, "hello". Puckered up when she saw that he was puckered. He planted her a nice kiss right on her lips busy in seemingly full conversation within the telephone call. She always enjoyed such sentiments from William ever since the beginning of their dating days. William continued with whatever it was that he was in discussion with Davis, in preparation for the evenings meal affairs because he acknowledged effortlessly that Journey was busy with the phone.

As Journey continued the call, she acknowledged her friend that she hadn't heard from in quite some time. Patricia, her friend on the other side of the phone, let her know that she planned to stop by and would be on her way in a bit. Journey agreed, "oh yes, yes... Please do. Stop on by. I'm sure we have a lot of catching up to do", Journey agreed. After a few "uhn huh, mm hmm and mm hmms" Journey then asked again to know for sureties, "So you're on your way?" Journey asked. "Okay, I look forward to your visit. We shall enjoy some crumpets and some chocolate European cookies dear. Come on by. I'll be waiting for you", she said. Patricia replied, "my pleasure", and then the ladies hung up their phones.

Patricia had already been in her car, close by and ready to stop by after making her pit stop by the gas station. Meanwhile, Journey continued to get relaxed in her home.

"Aah", she sighed as she looked for a place to sit down. William and his crew were preparing for tonight's small party that would be filled with a few guests from Journey's church possibly and a small amount of her interns from her company as well as, a small number of members from her nonprofit and some guests that were regulars at her bed & breakfast. Khalid often over saw some of her affairs for her from time to time since coming home.

As he was attending to the needs of the BnB or Bed & Breakfast, he interacts with the customers to assure guest satisfaction where his mother is busy with other endeavors and businesses. He put wind in his mother's ear that a few of the regular guests there began to fall on tough times. They even found difficulty in taking care of their basic needs. A few of the regulars had a challenging time with money for meals and everything due to the continuous acts of the government following the COVID-19 pandemic era. When the kitchen crew would cook any 2 meals of the day for the BnB for a fair price, Khalid would give them the meals practical free at times. He knew that the missing meals would not hurt his mother any nor her business not one bit. His mother was well to do. She wasn't always that way. It happened just recently.

Now a days new viruses have unleashed that the government doesn't even begin to know how to manage nor contain. These viruses are heard to have been around since the dinosaurs, due to the continuous melting of the polar ice caps.

William is mid-conversation with Davis, whom is in the kitchen stirring the pot. Davis and William are wearing the chef's hat, Chef Boyardee style. Journey saw the crew through the kitchen as she was pacing back and forth while on the phone in anticipation of being able to make the conversation brief. She could see through the kitchen's door as William swung open door the doors upon entry and exit. The rest of the kitchen crew were in the usual kitchen uniform.

The house smelt lovely from the smell of the fresh dumplings also known as pot stickers and the whatever else they were making. Journey had longed for jerked chicken 'n dumplings and she had hoped that it was on the menu. Just like her grandmother used to make. She had mentioned it to William some time before. She hoped that he had included it into the menu, but she liked to offer William kitchen freedom to do whatever it pleased him to do in the kitchen. That is where he worked best. In the kitchen William did what he needed to do as the aspiring top chef that he was.

William was very polite with Journey because this was a kitchen task that he could handle. He didn't feel the pressure. As a fact, there was less pressure on him to perform as there would have been if it were one of his regular kitchen gigs of cooking and preparing meals. He usually cooked and catered for celebrities, football players and all things high-end guests. Tonight, this was basically a family affair. No. This... This was just a simple party for Journey. Good times! Today was a good day.

William agreed to cater the party for her because he assumed that she was trying to raise money for more funding for her non-profit organization or trying to convert her guests into her church by holding a party. That was always how he would view her sentiments. He saw her as a self-proclaimed "gospel worker" as she called herself whenever she was what she called on a preaching mission or while shoving some words of the Bible down his throat. Journey saw it as sharing scriptures. He sees her as converting people into her cult. William giggled in his mind at the mere thought of it as his mind wandered away into one of her bible studies, he allowed her to give to him in recent pasts. Journey's thoughts are that, through enough preaching one-day William will change.

William had told Journey on many occasions that he only listens to her because he doesn't want to hurt her feelings. That he didn't know what to believe when it came to God, yadduh, yadduh, yadduh,yadduh the so on and the so forth. That was good enough for her.

That's simply the way that William viewed Journey's tactics and plannings, the visuals rang out through his mind, "Journey is converting her next cult members", were his antagonistic thoughts. He kept those in his head. He only wise cracked things if she asked him. He no longer wanted to question her thought processes nor her tactics. He just wanted to keep the peace and harmony that they had learned to build together.

William was a man that was very arrogant in his own right. He never really saw Journey in a positive light no matter what she would do, but he loved her anyway deep down in his soul, more importantly, in his heart. Anyone who knew them knew that the relationship was built on securities, not love. Journey, during her earlier stages of dating William, the relationship constantly went in to being in an on and off again stagnation, and then on and then off again with him, this went on for years. They were just two people who just wanted to be together and couldn't stand to see each other with anyone else.

Over her earlier years of William, she got used to dealing with the switching, some self-inflicted, and she learned to live with his ways for the longest time. Since their relationship in which was non-traditional, at the core, everyone who knew them got used to them.

Journey stopped trying to explain things to William. She stopped trying to involve William into her planning of things a long time ago. She slowly began to just let William know what she needed done and she expected him to accomplish just as she would request. He was free William to her. This sort of one sidedness was a learned behavior during her journey with William. She decided to learn this gesture once she began to realize that men hear what they want to hear not what you are telling them in actuality.

"Mom how was your day?", Khalid questions Journey as he pulls a chair out from their grand table for her. As he she was talking on the phone, he already had some tea, crumpets and coffee set up. He had one of the cooks to already arrange them on the table. "Busy", she shared as she got up from the chair of convenience that she was already sitting in, to set down into the much more comfortable grand dining room table chair that Khalid had arranged for her. He sat in another chair nearby her at the table.

"I took the day off son so that I could be home with you," she was reluctant to say. "My busy day never ends, and I hadn't seen you for most of your life. I wanted to take this time with you." she stared at him, "thank you my son for helping me from time to time where you could. I really appreciate you helping me to run my business affairs, and for keeping your commitment that you made to me in your youth. You kept your promising and actually came home... to live with me, my son. We cannot in no way make up for the time that was stolen from us in this horrible life situation committed against us through the corruption of the government agency of the state, the DHR and the child protective services. All that we can do is to work from here to rebuild us. Our relationship. I am glad that I had my affairs in order enough in my life as you have come home, so that I could have things that I am able to present to you." "Not a problem momma, I told you that I would come live with you. I am glad to be able to help you. There are so many things to catch up on momma. Things that are missing that I would like to connect with from my youth." "You know that I am glad that you are home. There will be nothing to come between us again.," Journey was able to state just before the doorbell rang." I will get it momma," Khalid says, and he goes for the door.

He opens it. Standing at the door was Patricia. "Is Journey here?" and out pops Journey quickly to the door in the greatest surprise. "This is quite the surprise," she invites Patricia in. Khalid attends to her coat and her hat. They are trying to knock the cool draft out of their bones and the snow out of Patricia's cold weather articles. The snow had begun to lightly fall in Miami, Florida due to pick up a bit more later in the day.

As Patricia is unbuttoning her load, she says to the two, "did you ever think that we would see the day when it would be cold and even snow... here in Miami, Florida this way?" "Child no..", Patricia stated, "I thought that hell would first freeze over". The trio laughed and sat down comfortably at the table to catch up. They all sat down to enjoy some tea or some coffee and some crumpets and some European cookies as well.

Journey introduced Khalid to Patricia. "Patricia this is my son Khalid ", she introduces. Patricia takes a good look at Khalid and says, "My Khalid...how much you've grown. I hadn't seen you since you were a little boy.' Journey corrected, "No that was my son Ishmael," Journey let her know. "Oh," Patricia said, "Well boy, your mother is a good person.," she said to Khalid. "I know" Khalid said, "I love my mother."

Patricia turned to Journey, "Girl and you've come so far. I just had to visit you. We hadn't always had the best of relationship because we had been going through our thing, but we are sisters. Girl since the military. Girl, I hadn't seen you since you left Alabama all them years ago. Bitch you were no longer in the military last I saw you", Patricia remembered, wrist on the hip and taken aback, "although I was. Chi-i-ild." Patricia's posture came back forward, and she leaned in and swiped at Journey with a feminine hand gesture before saying, "Girl, you made good for yourself. I just wish we could've kept up and kept more in contact from over all this lost time. So, what happened to you? Tell me the story of how you got this dashing son? He's so handsome," Patricia inquired.

"Well, if you really wanna know," Journey explained. "Yes, tell me girl. Yes, I really wanna know so tell me. Don't chou be holdin out. I wanna hear every little part. I mean I have my story too but yours seems," Patricia takes a moment to look around at the residence, "faaar more interesting." "Well only if you really wanna know", Journey explains with a wink at Patricia while taking a sip of her tea. "Oh, yea girl", Patricia sets her cup down and feminine swipes again. She picks her teacup up once more, she says, "Yes. I really wanna know", Patricia says gazing into Journey with intent meanwhile slowly putting her sipped cup down because her attention gleamed off it and the hot contents within it. "Well, okay," Journey says, **"If you really wanna understand my story I have to take you back to the beginning...** of my journey", she stated as she took a sip into her glass of tea... one finger up before setting her teacup down.

A series of flashbacks from her younger times in Alabama flash readily through Journey's mind and her memories begin.

Chapter 2

DALE COUNTY ALABAMA (LATE 2005)

It was a carefree, worry-free day on an extended journey down to the southern hemisphere of the United States. State territories in the deep south, most southern of the Mason Dixon line for Journey. The Mason-Dixon is the line that separates the north from the south. The line goes straight across the U.S., the line goes across and Kentucky, being in the north and Tennessee being in the south.

As she was driving down southbound on the interstate-95, she felt freedom. To Journey a car always meant freedom. She was once again in the wind and free from her tormenter. The chains felt broken as she put miles between herself and her recent past dropping down out of the state of Maryland. As she had done many times before she had her young son Ishmael along for the ride. He was with her and by her side. Ishmael was quietly sleeping in the back seat of her silver mustang underneath the piles of their belongings.

The only time that Ishmael was ever not on a journey at Journey's side, was if he was in the care of a family member or relative when she would go on her very demanding in schedule aviation jobs. Initially when Journey began to leave her son with relatives for work, it was the hardest thing that she ever had to do in her life. Even to share her young child with the other parent, it absolutely tore her to tears. Eventually Journey came sort of used to it. She was groomed to be a parent since her youth by caring for her younger siblings, so she never ever grew totally detached from her son, ever.

In the early days of Ishmael's life, she never left Ishmael with his biological father because he was not available into Ishmael's life until later in his life. Carl Ripken, Ishmael's biological father, no matter how much Journey tried, Carl refused to get involved. He made himself unavailable to be a part into Ishmael's life. In Ishmael's early days, he was not ready to claim her boy, Ishmael, as his child, being from his own loins. From what Journey observed about the guy, he was simply fine living this fantasy life.

Journey was a strong woman. She was older than Carl by a fragment of years, so she did not feel the need to burst his bubble about things just yet. From her observations into his Facebook page and his wife's page, she felt as if the woman stole Carl from her anyway when she was only two months pregnant with Ishmael and still in the military. From her observations, he didn't want to be involved in the life of her son nor did she want for him to be involved with her son at this precious time in Ishmael's life. She didn't feel the need to continue in pursuits of trying to burst Carl's bubble. She did not want to be the cause of any outside interference into his fantasy world, into his daydream. Call it foolish or naïve. Call it what you want to. Journey called it freedom. Of course, the fantasy had to end for Carl at some time, but this is not yet that part of the story.

Journey had been in quite some risky situations before having a child, but those situations could not even compare to the terror of being a mom and leaving your child into the care of someone else. Not even for one moment. That is not how Journey was raised to be. She was not raised to be an unfit parent nor was she raised to even neglect her child(ren).

Journey grew up a military brat inside of a tight knit Navy family community. The neighborhood was a little too tight knit in Journey's opinion. Therefore, he was always at her side. Going on contract was the only thing that she knew how to do to effectively as a means. It was better than an alternative way to make supportive income for them both, being that the daddy did not bother to be around.

Journey held fantasies at times about what her life would be like had she taken on a few gigs prior to conceiving Ishmael. What if she had become a stripper. She felt that she would be a damned good one because her body build was thick.

Journey memory recalls hanging out at a stripper bar. Her male friend brought her by the club to give things a try. They stopped at the door man, who lowered his glasses at Journey because he wanted to know who Dave was bringing with him into the club and not paying any money to get past his doors. He lifted his glasses because he wanted to take a good look at the merchandise. The man running the house tells one of the girls, Precious, to go up and show the ladies how use that pole. Owner, "uh Precious", he clapped his hands at the girl, "Go up and show these ladies how. To work that pole bitch. Let them see what chou got. Huh boo." "Yes daddy", Precious responded back. "Uh somebody hand me a bottle of that spray and a paper towel. Yall know I gots to wipe this pole down before doing my thing". Precious had climbed up the stage and was pulling her G-string out on her derriere because it had managed to ride too far up by the time, she had made it to the stage. The ladies had already tossed her a bottle of that disinfectant spray and she quickly wiped the pole down. The stripper music began to play, when the base dropped. Precious was up that pole, working that pole and doing her thing. All the girls were cheering and jeering breaking out dollar bills to place into her strings. Precious was the best stripper in the house whom they became good friends later. Dave stood up to hype the house up, "Now that's how you work that pole!" Aah the memories fade. Everything fades in the end.

Being an aviation contractor empowered her, though. It was an honest living. At times she felt like a pirate. Traveling from here to there. One of Journey's favorite pirate movies was old Captain Jack Sparrow and the gang in the "Pirates of the Caribbean" movie. Being an aviation contractor, it was her strength, as well as her weakness at times. It caused a lot of her future problems in her life eventually I tell you that but... It was a life that she loved. Unavoidable. After some time of having to do it, leaving Ishmael with a care provider... eventually, she got used to it.

She is somewhere in Florida quite some miles and hours later from one of the chocolate cities of America called Baltimore, that she had rode down to Alabama after residing there for a short amount of time. As Journey is driving along on her , she realized that she was driving too far because her legs were getting waay too tired from stepping on the gas pedal. Her back was beginning to bother her from sitting so long within the contour of the bucket seats, and Ishmael was trying to find the best arrangement for falling asleep amidst their things.

Journey's fatigue led her to pull over to take some rest at a rest stop and to refresh on a nice hot cup of hot coffee. She also thought while scanning through the isles to pick up something sweet to keep her mouth working & busy so that she would not fall asleep behind the wheel of the car while driving. It was late. She thought about her son, as well as her self's safety first. This was something that had always rang in Journey's mind since her life and times that she spent within the US Army military, "safety first." She also kept in mind that she also had her young son's life in her hands.

While pit stopped Journey thought that she would ask the people where she was. She could not figure out her location. The people looked like locals to the area. The locals were helpful, where Journey thought she was in Alabama, she found that she had overshot her travels and had found that she had wandered into the state of Florida. 'Oh." she thought to herself in her head, 'I guess that military map reading class didn't really pay off.' She shrugged the mishap off in her mind.

While following the next directions given to her by the locals, she began to recall events of her life while in Maryland before coming into this game of chance and overshooting her destination. One special night she went to a popular bar in the area and performed poetry, open mic night. As well she admired other performers and took part in listening to their performances. That is where she met Spivey.

There he was, kicked back in the cut, taking a listen at the poetry going on at the moment. He had his legs extended and legs crossed. He wore dress slacks checkered; they were high water. He wore black socks that came above his ankle in which he rolled down and dress shoes. He kept his hands in his pants pockets wearing a brown kangol styled hat on his head with the brim tilted down to one side of his face. His lips were big, and they had the black outline to them like most in his culture had. A Trinidadian. His blazed was pushed outward, supported by his hands in his pockets sitting down. As the poet was freely walking around with the mike and spitting poetry, he got the entire crowd to rub their fingers together supporting a poetic gesture. When Spivey looked up that's when he noticed her. She had just casually walked in that night into the fun and found her place among the crowd.

He and her hit it off well at first. He was from Trinidad, she did not hold that against him. Instead, she viewed him to learn a bit more about the culture of the west indies from his point of view. As she had already learned what she had just despised about the culture during her youth while growing up back in Texas. Journey recalled her stepfather being very strict with her. Almost militant. Also at times, very inappropriate with her. Journey chalked it up to the culture.

Journey quit her job at Aberdeen Proving Grounds Maryland as part of a road crew, due to no longer having childcare for her son Ishmael available to her. She had made the tough decision to move in with her friend who resided in Baltimore. At least she thought Spivey was her friend, while she happened to take a job and work a bit further north, in Hagerstown, Maryland. She decided to take an aviation contract job position located in Hagerstown, Maryland in which she found herself laid off from shortly thereafter.

You see Journey had just driven down from out of Baltimore, MD after finishing an aviation contract that she had to quit & after a long fight with her boy toy, whom was not a particularly good toy, the man Spivey.

Spivey was not as free as Journey when it came to sexual relations. One time when she tried to give him pleasures to his genitals with her mouth, he was not able to relax and enjoy the moment. During the slurping and spitting and the skin to skin, playing. Journey gently pulled at him with her teeth, she thought that he would at some point grab the back of her head and cause things to get real erotic. Actually. She looked forward to it, but he was different than other lovers that she had experienced from her past. When he took too long to grab her head or get involved during the session, she looked up at him to see if he was enjoying what she was doing to him.

Instead, he had his eyes closed tight and he was really flinched up. She took a bit of time out as she slowed down her actions to observe if there was any indication of joy in his foot work, but his feet were clenched up too. Journey thought to herself, "okay..." as she got off him. This grown ass man looked like a child being molested by her. Journey asked him about the experience, and he said that he did not really like it much.

Another time with Spivey, she tried to sneak in on the shower and just get in with him since they had already done things together, and in her attempt to make things fun and to engage into things interesting in the shower with him. Journey quietly entered the bathroom stark naked, and she had just dropped her towel. Spivey heard someone come in he thought.

As he was rubbing the soap suds all over his body, he was lost in thought of all the alarm system orders that he had to put in for that day. Journey pulled the shower curtain back on him very slowly in preparation to get into the shower and join in with him when he took a swipe at her nose quickly as if in attempt to hit her. His knuckles grazed Journey's nose. He swiped at her as if to say, back her off his privacy in the shower as if she was a sex offender or something.

There were a couple of other bad moments experienced by him, but Journey was not willing to stick around and figure out the dramatic issues on a grown man's life. She had finally made the decision that this was time to move on. Both she and Ishmael had to make their exit, you know, leave. She sorts of, kicks herself out of his house. Spivey's slightly younger than him, brother tried to talk with her through the heat of the situation. He tried to talk her out of it. He let her know that his brother was a difficult person but where was she going to go with her young son? Letting her know that her brother needed love, but he just did not know how to deal with women after the passing of their mother which left them the house. She continued her fit, slewing her things into the yard only to finally place her son and things inside of the vehicle and leave. She did not mind the yard, she thought to get out of the house and away from him as quickly as she could. She packed her son and then herself inside of her silver Grand Am and then fish tailed up out on his yard. All his brother could see was taillight, dust and peel out smoke.

Of all the trips that Journey had made... In her mind, this trip was an extended one as she had never driven so far south before. The only thing that she had to go off was a road map that she learned to read earlier on in her life while serving time in the military how to read.

Journey and her team meet up and they have to meet at the rendezvous point. They are all in kevlar, flack vest, military boots. Full battle rattle. Their weapons by their side. Their muzzles suppressed of course to prevent friendly fire or accidentally discharging a round. They are all standing around with a map and a compass trying to figure out there current position as opposed to where they need to be. They work as a team and discuss their location and then they head that way. They make their point as a team and in good timing.

Before her Baltimore friend, she was involved with a co-worker on her travel team from work. His name was Derrick. She recalled hanging with Derrick while living a nice life. She was living with Derrick & other co-workers in a nice big house out on Orchid Beach, New Jersey off Jersey shores. This home belonged to a guy that he turned his home into a vacation rental. Within his home he had pictures around his residency of himself and his interactions with the pope. It was a lovely home, a nice sized place. A nice sized island right smack dab in the middle of his huge kitchen.

She recalled getting drunk at the island in the kitchen and singing the song "Gold Digger" featuring Jamie Foxx & Kanye and making a pun, a play on some of the words of the song in her drunken state. Then Derrick reached out for the bottle and took the bottle of alcohol away from her because that was the only way that he could think of that people were going to get any sleep in the house. She was singing too much, it was too late and most observably, she was singing too loud. The entire crew had an exceedingly early day to make it in to work on time for the next day. Derrick was in no mood for her drunken silliness, and he was extremely tired from having drinks himself prior to hearing from her. Although Derrick and Journey were very fond of each other, they took care of each other. As team members out contracting on the road, more than likely with no relatives around them for support. While out on the road and on contracts, contractors learned to watch out for each other. Most were prior military anyway.

As she was exhausted from her drive and did not realize far back at some time ago within her daydream that she should have had taken the I-85 South route down from Maryland and then ended up on some back roads in Alabama. Journey learned this travel route later in life and experience. She had vivid memories of the sounds of her father telling her to, "live a little you might learn some more."

Journey's mind wandered along the drive. It was a way for her to kill time along her long drive. She recalled at times when she would try from day to day to engage into conversations with Spivey, he seemed irritable. Journey could see that her and Ishmael's stay had somehow taken away his peace of mind away. He had a comfortable home, but Journey had finally reached her breaking point with it.

Upon her arrival to work one morning at Hagerstown she was let go. She immediately got on the horn to achieve another position from her aviation recruiter. Two days later she as approved for another aviation contract position which happened to be in Dale County Alabama and mentally, she was on the move.

After work, Journey went to Spivey's home for her final argument with the guy. He had some sort of complaint about her son Ishmael who was simply being a kid. The Baltimore guy told her to get out. Journey did not waist one moment. She slew all their things, both her and her son Ishmael's things, all over his lawn of Spivey's home, as her young son Ishmael stood on the lawn watching and waiting on his mother's direction of what to do next. They had decided to go their separate ways.

She had a memory recall of when he had helped her to transport her things over to his house. The ride down the beltway. He got mad with her for going her own way and not following hm with his driving down the highway. She took and alternative route. At that time in her life, he seemed like a guy who meant well and a caretaker. She later learned that he could not handle such pressures.

The further Journey got down the road, her son piled in the backseat of the car with all their belongings, the closer she got to her past. She felt the air and took deep breaths of freedom! It was in the air.

While driving along the busy highway in the nighttime... lights were in her eyes. She attempts at the dimming effect of the rear-view mirror. Just there after she manages to find and exit at Cottondale, Florida. She asks the people at the gas station where she is? The people let her know that she is in somewhere Florida. She thinks to herself "Florida?? I thought that I was in Alabama...you mean I passed Alabama". She grabs a road map and realizes that she overshot her destination. She somehow heads up a road called Highway-234 heading north for Dothan / Ozark, Alabama by way of Cottondale, Florida.

By the morning time she makes it to a convenience store. She realizes that her funds are running low and so is her gas. She lowers her head in realization that she must call Spivey, the man that she had driven soo far away from to begin another life in Alabama.

She pulled over to the nearest pay phone and she gave him a call. She let him know that she was not far now. "Where are you?" he asked. "I am not that far away from my destination, now. Actually. I overshot my destination; I went too far. I got lost. I drove all the way down into Florida & I need to go back up," she shared, "to Alabama". She let him know that she was out of money and that she needed a hundred dollars. He took a deep sigh out of aggravation and then he agreed to send it to her, and he wired it to her via Western Union. She was on the road again. Before leaving the grocery stop at Cottondale, Florida, she picked up a few scratch offs. She ended up winning enough to pay for a motel room for a few nights and to eat. Scored. She thought the money will at least hold her over until she could get her employer to extend her an advance.

She pulled into the first local hotel that she saw out of Dale County Ozark, Alabama. She paid for a room for herself and her son. Then she headed for the gas station not too far up the road. She was in search of a sitter as she had to be at work on Monday.

As she pulled into the gas station in Dale County Ozark Alabama, that's when a white van full of passengers pulled up in front of her at the same time. The driver jumped out & stated, "oooh you cute'. She held a short conversation with him letting him know that she had just come down from Baltimore like just now. He told her, "That's where we from. We from there. From Jersey." His passenger came back to the car, so he had to go. He asked Journey for her number, and she gave it to him.

Chapter 3

I NEED A BABYSITTER

Journey enters the gas station; Khalid drove off and went on his way with his seemingly passenger filled up with no more seating available, passenger van.

It was a normal sized conveniently located gas station that motorists could quickly get to while riding down Highway-231 of Dale County to Ozark, Alabama. Highway 231 is one of the crossroads of America. This highway routes all the way up to as far as Clarksville, Tennessee and beyond. All the way up to St. Johns, Indiana and down more southern to Panama City, Florida.

Journey learned later in her life that, evidentially she had visited the state some time ago while serving in the military, while accompanying a friend to the area. She understood very little about the different roads that she was traveling at that time in her life. A friend later in her life recalled to her the moments from when she had formerly visited the area earlier in her life to remind her of the area., as she was sharing with them her experience.

She could not ever picture herself living in a place such as Alabama. Being that she was from California and all. She even had friends in her association that would never dream of stepping foot on such soil of a place like Alabama. Like that of many of the travel adventures that Journey had been on in her life her associations would never step foot.

"We'd listened to stories, girl", Patricia confirmed as Journey was explaining. "Girl, now you know that I am from D.C. myself child and I would have never dreamed that I would step my foot into such a place. But you know, life leads you into experiencing some things". "Just the same", Journey said. Spreading her arms for her current residence, "I have now become a southern girl. This south is way different than the wild, wild west side where I grew up".

Journey's sentiments were just the same, as her associates, yet her circumstances and her decisions in her given money-making situations had changed her level of chance taking that she was willing to take in her life to make a bit of bread in her life. Like many entrepreneurs and even old money, established, she took her gamble.

Journey enjoyed gambling. The game of chance, it gets surprising sometimes at where life is willing to take you. Journey at times in her life visited the local casinos in Miami prior to the nuclear fallout that caused the weather change. She often visited Calder Casino and Hialeah casino. A time or two she would visit the High Life off 36th Street at Lajeune Road. There were many more in the area, like the guitar in Broward and the lesser one at the Dolphin's stadium but she didn't gamble as much in Florida. She'd rather frequent Tunica and Biloxi in her youth. Or even the gas stations at Louisiana or at times even Delaware Downs. Yet, this is not that part in the story.

So, there she was, looking for a babysitter out of Ozark, Alabama. Yuck!

As she enters the gas station, she encounters the attendant at that time and lets her to know that she is search of a babysitter from her son. She lets the lady know what brings her into town and that she will be needing someone to look after her young son. The lady tells her that she knows of a woman who sits in town. She picks up the phone and gives the local babysitter woman a call.

"Hello Sheree", she says in a loud husky Alabama twanged, country, assured voice, "I got a woman here just come into town and gone be working up at that there uh helicopter place up the road. She is needin a sitter for her youngin. Are you open to sitting? Or do you know of anybody who is up for the job?". She then carries on saying "uh huh, aah ha, yeah, okay. Sure", she holds on and grasps the receiver to the phone, she then whispers, "you'll be needing that sitter on tomorrah, right?" Journey shakes her head for yes, up and down. She gets back to the conversation on the phone, and she says," yes, she'll be needing for you to sit on tomorrahh...sure will...will do, well I will give her your number so that she can go up some time today to meetcha. ...okay then, bye for now. I'll holler."

She ends the call by hanging up the phone and passes on Sheree's number to Journey. "Thank you soo much', she replies at the attendant as she is gathering some things for herself and for Ishmael to snack on before finding them a place to eat dinner.

After Journey unpacks the car and settles into her motel room, she notices a shadow of a man in the background while doing her hair in the motel mirror who is not there. Upon seeing the shadow, it quickly goes away. She thought that she was losing her mind. She made a few attempts to recreate the shadow but was unsuccessful. She decided to dismiss what she saw and to continue with her life.

She gathers up Ismael and heads on over to Ms. Sheree's place. Upon arriving there she notices that the place is okay. She has more than a few children over, she takes note that the woman also has a lot of bugs crawling around, commonly referred to as roaches. The bugs made it difficult to focus on conversation when in conversation, so does her best to pretend that the bugs do not exist, Journey pays the crawlers no never mind, well she is a bit desperate in her situation. First day in town with a work obligation to fulfill the following day and not enough time to further look around, she is desperately in need of a sitter, and quickly so, she had to work with what she had until she could position herself a better babysitter situation. Before leaving the house, she meets Sheree's daughter Latasha and her friend, and they head on back over to the motel.

Come Monday morning, she drops Ishmael over to the sitter Ms. Sheree's house on her way off for work at the local helicopter company in the area. Journey managed to pack Ishmael's things with everything that she thinks he will need throughout his day.

Thank you, Ms. Sheree, for taking care of my child for me while I go away to work".

"Now I do not know what time I will be getting off because aviation is really demanding, and they do not usually just let you get off from work at the drop of the dime or because we just want to. Since it is my first week, I do not even know my schedule yet", she got lost in her thoughts of what she just shared. Which made her wonder from time to time why she was still in the game. Was it the thrill of the game? "Okay", Journey begins her walking away, "I shall be back soon. Thank you, Ms. Sheree, for taking care of my child for me while I go away to work". Journey was forever grateful for doing what she does. Managing the welfare of children. It's takes especially unique personality to do so.

Journey briefed Ms. Sheree so that she could have an idea into her work lifestyle. Journey wasn't what she was used to. Unless she babysat for unique career-oriented individuals. She briefly gave her information into her ways, into her life and into lifestyle as she is living the life as a single parent having an extremely limited support system with a young child on her arms.

In the long haul, Ms. Sheree turns out to be a reliable source of support over her stay in the Dale County area. She becomes someone that she could really rely on and to trust to help her with her childcare provider needs for an extended period over time.

Chapter 4

I CAN FEEL A LAYOFF COMING

Today is the first day. Journey meets her onsite recruiter. She meets a few co-workers, all good ole boys. She meets one lady there on her team. This lady loved to butter up all the co-workers providing them with candy and sweet tooth treats and such. Katy walks over to the table where the crew has their gear and tools set up with a bag of candy assortments. "Good morning, everyone", Katy says." Good morning, Katy", everyone greets her back but at different time intervals. Different fellers from the different crews started to pass by the table for whatever the reason. Whether it was to head to the restroom or to stop by the tool room on the way or just to start very short polite conversation with Katy before getting to their jobs. You could hear the busy buzzing of the morning at the workplace, as the workplace came to life. Little by little, as each employee as well as department came in and got together.

Journey just loved to simply do her job. She wasn't one of a social butterfly. Journey was in her own world as usual to the rear of the aircraft working on a rather complicated harness assembly. She didn't bother to ask for any help or input from anyone because she was unaware of the point when she should ask, and no one bothered to come up to her and ask if she was doing okay. She wasn't experienced enough yet as an electrical assembler in her skill set, although she was prior military.

One time while Journey was at the job, she had left a heated soldering iron on sitting on the seat of the aircraft. She didn't leave any kind of a warning or anything, which would have been a courtesy, and she headed for the parts room where she soon met a fellow named Jerry. Jerry was the parts room guy who handed out the tools and the parts. Jerry and Journey later ended up spending a lot of time together and they later became longtime friends.

As Journey was on her way back with the part, she could see Tom in an in-depth decision making, peer focused conversation with Katy. Journey held her hand out and began the sprawl to warn Tom against it, as he had stuck his bun out to cop a squat for a sit. She was too far across the helicopter to warn her co-worker Tom that the iron was hot. He was attempting to help Katy out with her project in question. He sat right down on the hot soldering iron and immediately sprung back up and he grabbed his derriere. He yelled loud while holding on to his derriere. Angrily he looked around for the culprit. He took note of Journey is scurrying over to his way and is in sincere apology to him, "I am soo sorry Jerry, I didn't think that anyone wouldn't see it. In the least check it to see if it's hot. You couldn't smell the hot? The heat? Coming from the iron...", she takes a deep breath in, "It's a soldering iron Jerry." She is shocked that he didn't bother to look to see if that tool was cooled before sitting down. She could not believe that he managed to not see it. Jerry is still looking at her with the eyes of disbelief. Which quickly fringed. He would try to kill her but his beambaawhacka was hot. He was holding on to his hide for dear life due to the pain. He slowly turned and he walked off, removing himself from the situation.

The days went by quickly. There was the daily routine of performing the job and the daily meetings. The helicopter company had a crew in the building working on some cabling for their new internet system they were having installed. One of the workers on the crew caught Journey's eye. His name was Tee, and when Tee finally approached Journey, she could feel the winds of seduction blowing her hair back. There was magnetism between the two and they rarely lost sight of each other, other than to work. Journey found herself caught up talking with him often. He took up much of her break times and her me times.

Through her whirlwind romancing period together with Tee... he would visit her over to her motel room. A few times she found difficulty paying her motel room and he would foot the bill. He acknowledged her little guy, Ishmael, a handsome child. He immediately took a liking towards Ishmael. He did not want to see the little feller, Ishmael, suffering not one bit.

Chapter 5

SNIFFING OUT EACH OTHER

Journey pulled up in her silver Grand Am with her son Ishmael in the back seat. She gathers her son from out of the car and she heads up the lawn to what Journey thought would be Khalid's house, but he was living with his mother. It turned out to be Lauren's house. Journey was holding her son Ishmael by the hand, when the two made it up the porch.

Khalid is there sitting on the porch playing on his flip phone awaiting her arrival. His mother Lauren states, "Oh! You plannin a guest?", hand on her hip as she exited for outside with a belt in her hand. At the moment Khalid was in a little bit of hot water with his mother for putting her through hell. He had just gotten out of prison and now being on house arrest, at no place other than her home. He introduces his mother to Journey," Ma this is Journey, Journey this is my mother".

His mother Lauren comes out the screen door just to get a good look at the guests but goes back into the house to continue whatever task it was that she had been doing prior to the interruption. She is in the home with the house door wide open and viewing everyone through the screen door. She wants to ensure that Khalid, her son does not leave the porch without telling her where it is that he intends on going. His mother comes out the doorway and extends her hand out to Journey, "hi I'm Lauren ", shook Journey's hand and knelt to get a good look at Ishmael, "are you bad?" she says to Ishmael with a wince. Ishmael hides behind Journey.

"My mother used to have a daycare" he says to Journey while biting his nails. Journey then takes notice to all the tattoos that Flex has all over his body. Especially the ones on his kneck. His tattoos were quite a few but not too many as she had seen men have too much ink. His were just enough, enough to her liking. She would later find that to be rather sexy as she loved tattoos. It's just that at that moment, something appeared to be very wrong with him. Upon her initial judging of him from viewing him, she thought that he was very sick.

She then thought to take a look, and to take very intricate notes of his very athletic, sculpted body type. That she liked. He seemed to be of a very athletic specimen, but why was he soo skinny? She couldn't 't get that thought out of her head. He was light skinned but his mother was dark skinned. At the time that she took note of him she thought that he looked rather sick. She didn't know if he had AIDS or what was going on with him.

"Yea, I used to run a daycare out of my house", Lauren chimed in. "How are you?', she said as she walked back into her home. Journey smiled. Lauren let the two be. She let them talk. As she walked back into the house, she sternly told Khalid, "Don't you leave that porch". "I'm not!" he responded back. He began biting his nails again. His posture was crouched over, elbows relaxing on his knees with big high top tennis shoes on his feet.

"So", Khalid began to ask, "you said you just came down here from Maryland?". "Yea, yes, we did. I had got lost on the drive back there. I never been this far south before outside of the military." Khalid shared, "we moved down here from Jersey. We been down here for quite a few years now". She couldn't help but to notice Khalid's mannerisms as he spoke. He shook his head when he talked. His held his body up, when taking a break from his nail biting. His head shaking gave him his own personal way of speaking with swagger. He was very sure of himself when he talked. But he always bit his nails.

"I just got out. I did time in prison", he let Journey know, throwing his head around assuredly when he spoke. He sort of looked at her but looked past her as he shared. As if he was a bit in memory or in thought of something. He spoke like a northerner. Sort of like a nice tough guy, not a macho one. "Prison?", Journey responded startled. Not something to be expected from someone she would be conversing with. She quickly thought of family members in her head who may have had the same experience on her father's side of the family, but Journey didn't want to be an early judge. She proceeded on in the conversation to ask, "Well how long was you in there?" I did two years" he replied, "and I'm still on papers for another year".

Journey took notice to how light skinned his complexion was in comparison to his mothers. Journey being from California and all. A state where everybody is mixed with something, she asked Khalid, "Are you mixed with anything?"" Italian. My father is half Italian", he shared with Journey.

Lauren came back to the entry way, to the screen at the door, "What time are you supposed to be at work?" He stated, "I'm leaving now", turning to Journey he asked, **"can you give me a ride to work? I work at Perdue"**, "Where's that?" Journey asked. "The chicken plant", he said. "I really don't know Journey said. When you saw me, I literally just pulled into the area, even into the state". "I'll show you how to get there", Khalid said, "The plant is in Dothan".

Chapter 6

THE SCARE WHILE TAKING KHALID TO WORK

The only reason that Journey stopped by his place and even got into this situation of taking Khalid to work in the first place is because she enjoyed his smooth introduction upon her arriving to the gas station. It was an intro that she would never forget for some reason throughout the rest of her life. "Oooh you cute", she recalled the conversation in her mind. She thought to herself, this one has swaggerrr.

Being that Journey was more of a city girl, she didn't understand certain traffic lights, regulations initially in the south. As she was driving along down the highway 231, she took notice of a light that in the north and out west were used for fire houses and firefighters. It was used to let traffic know that the fire engines were coming out fast. In Journey's observation of the dinky light, she didn't see not fire house, no fire engines or nothing. She did however take note of a four-way intersection. She was driving at top speed in her silver Grand Am. Speed limit posted was 55-mph, but Journey was going a little faster than that.

She kept in mind that she had lives in her hand. Her baby boy seated in the back.

She asked Khalid, "Is that a stop light?", because the light was yellow and flashing with a circle around it like at the fire station. She took note of vehicles stopped and the light from all sides. Khalid just looked at her, with a look that was a dare. Journey still wasn't quite too sure, and she began to become confused, "do I keep going?", she said aloud. Khalid told her, "Yeah", as he was still looking at her. The look and demeanor in his face looked as if he was placing Journey on a dare, to see if she would go through the light. The moment grew intense for Journey as she was flying down a hill with limited time to stop, as she was completely unsure of what that light meant.

It wasn't until she saw a vehicle enter the intersection from the opposing direction that she realized that this light meant to stop!!! She slammed on her brakes extra hard and finally came to a stop at the light. The force was enough to put flat spots on her tires. She looked over at Khalid, she was upset. She always thought, safety first. She had her 4-year-old son in the back seat.

He gave a light laugh as he shrugged the event off. He went back to biting his nails. He wanted to see if Journey would do it. If she would run through that light, and if she did do it, what would be the result after words.

She was soo angry with him that she began to drive fast and meaningful. She couldn't wait to drop him off to Perdue or the chicken plant or to wherever it is that he said that it worked. An incident that Khalid took so lightly, became a defining moment later in their relationship. A thing she could never forget. She had made her judgment about him. A judgment that would later haunt.

She didn't call him back nor answer his phone calls for at least 6 months although he tried, and he tried to contact her with all his heart. He was nervous but he fell for her. **Journey decided that Khalid did not value his life.** Well, she valued hers and even more, she valued the life of her 4-year-old son who was dependently seated in the back seat of the car.

This very incident was one of the causes of many delays in realizations throughout their relationship. However, Khalid was able to realize the time lost, although he didn't know the reason, and he, as well, possessed the ability to hold on to the realization sooner than Journey was able to.

Chapter 7

"Journey Meets the Music Producer"

"One day I was out showing off my cd that I had recording", Journey mentions. "You a recording artist?", Patricia chimes in, "oh yes, I remember when we were in the military you said that you were singing with a band. Sorry I never came to enjoy one of yawls recordings ", Patricia said while taking a sip of her tea. "It's okay girl. It is nothing that I ever aspired to anyway as you can see. My dreams and desires changed immensely following that summer".

While Journey was out, she ran into Suga. Suga took a listen Journey's recordings. "Your hot", he said, "but you could use some better producers." "You think so?", Journey replied, "I've been told that one time or another. I used to record out of Philly with a producer and out of Clarksville, Tennessee. I considered recording out of New York, but we'll see" Suga let her know, "I know one I got chou". "Okay cool", she said. "I've sold my cds out of my trunk up and down the east coast. Mostly so that I could have money for gas and not be stranded anywhere. Well, okay...", Journey was open to what Suga was letting her know. "Matter of fact, I am on my way over there to see him now if you wanna follow me over there," he shared, "then after that I am going over to this rental company to try to rent me an apartment. It just doesn't make no sense to keep paying on these hotels around here when an apartment is way cheaper. Right now, I'm staying with my girl", he said. " But I need a place of my own.", he was committed to it. Journey let him know that she too was interested in an apartment. She made plans to tag along with after the studio session.

Inside the studio Journey met with Silas, the music producer. Silas extended his hand and they all sat around meeting and greeting. There were a few other artists in the studio at the time. The artists were making their way out because their recording sessions were over for the day, so they were making their way out.

Silas had on a leather jacket because the day had cooled. He drove a fully loaded van. Journey had no idea as to why. She thought, some guys just love vans. He had a small afro, and he wore sandals, which many would refer to as Jesus sandals. HHe walked with a walking stick. Not for support or anything. It's just that it became customary for him to walk with it.

Silas was sitting at his studio track station mixing down tracks and listening to beats, allowing for Journey to hear the type of sounds that he generally messes with. Silas also took a listen at Journeys cd. He liked what he heard but he felt the same as Suga, she needed a better production team. Journey was attracted a little bit to his beats. It was enough to keep Journey coming back from time to time in attempts to record.

After all the listening, and giggling and the sharing, Journey and Suga made way to go to the rental agency to check into their applications for an apartment. Suga dapped out Silas, scheduling a meeting for next time and he shook hands with Journey on the way out.

Chapter 8

"I CAN FEEL A LAYOFFS IN DALE COUNTY"

Journey had come into the eyes of the parts room guy while gathering parts for her project at work. His name was Jerry. Jerry became very fond of Journey because she was interesting, and she was not a local from the area. Jerry was a family man, and a very southern Bonaventure as well. His ways were deeply southern rooted. He spoke with a haughty southern accent. She sat in the parts room a time or two with him to enjoy lunch in his company.

One day Journey goes to work. The company calls a meeting to bitch about what they are not happy about. Parts coming in slow. Workers having to make work. Journey and every contractor there could feel a layoff coming on. Jerry put a word in her ear and directed for her to apply to an aircraft company out in Houston County. She did just that.

The co-worker that worked directly next to her that himself was pretending to work, did not care for the atmosphere there. He heard the buzz in the air. He knew how the men in a male dominated industry labeled women in aviation with their male domineering ideas.

He asked journey if she wanted to go out contracting with him as his partner. He let her know that she would not have to work, just tend to mostly his needs if she'd liked, unless she just wanted to work. He saw the fragility of her being a woman in this sort of industry. He thought that she was good looking. He saw that she was a woman that could do the same sort of work that a man could do, and he thought of her as knowledgeable with it too. He just was wanting to be a friend and he wanted to take care of her and try to cut her a break from the hustle and bustle of life.

He was a decent looking man who meant well, but Journey politely declined his offer. He let her know that he was getting ready to leave. The gentleman stated, "I'm getting ready to leave tomorrow. You are welcome to come with me." Journey didn't believe him because she had no understanding of no one just quits like that.

When tomorrow came, he was not there. The layoffs had begun. Journey was of the first on the chopping block. Journey was devastated. She had not yet grown

Chapter 9

"Journey & Khalid Meet Again"

Journey was laid off from her job, no less than the time that she entered the doors and began to fiddle with her toolbox her recruiter comes over to her and let her know that her contract had ended and that she needed to bring her toolbox. Her onsite recruiter had to walk her to the door. Journey was a bit of disappointed at the action. She managed to gather herself and her things with the news.

After loading her toolbox into her vehicle Journey visits over to Sheree's with her son Ishmael. She lets her know that she doesn't now have a plan. She asks her to hold on to Ishmael for the night. Sheree agrees to be help. This buys her a little thinking time until she can figure out a new plan.

Journey pulls into a local parking lot to go to sleep. While she is deep in thought and in frustration a little van pulls up full of passengers. She doesn't quite perceive in the moment who is in the minivan when it pulls over. Khalid gets out at the driver's side, and he asks Journey if she was alright? "Are you okay?", he asks. Journey begins vivid memory recalls of the trip south; she remembers giving him the ride to his job and decides that she doesn't want to deal with him at all. She is agitated with him and begins to be rude. It is her attempts to get rid of him quickly, she relates, "I'm fine. I'm good." He looks at her strangely because he doesn't believe her, "you sure?". "Yeah. I'm sure. I'm good", she replies. "O--kay", he says.

Not knowing what else to say, he backs away from her slowly, still concerned because her situation looks distressed, but he gets back in the van and drives off.

Journey didn't know it at the time because she was so filled with anger, that she missed her one opportunity. He was her lifeline. She realized this later in the story but at that time in her life because she was blinded by emotions. This little fent would have been a way for her to avoid all the trials that she had to go through. It would have been the uncomplicated way out. Why would her journey need to go that way? Who really wants things easy anyway.

Nighttime fell. Journey knew nothing about the area. She was an ex-soldier military soldier that slept outside on a cot, in a sleeping bag with strange, wooded creatures for a living. Creatures like snakes and giant wooded hunter spiders, and recluses and tarantulas and cow patties. It was nothing for her to spend a night in car. Journey had managed to doze off in the mist of her worrying. She even considered simply taking her son up to her father and his girlfriend's place in Chicago for a while.

As Journey was in her slumber in the quiet country town, a pair of bright lights flashed into her face that awoke her. It was the Dale County police. Journey rolled down her window to acknowledge the officer that approached her vehicle. "Can I help you Officer?", Journey initiated conversation. After the usual questioning of license and vehicle registration the officer asked her, "what are you doing here?". Journey let the officer know that she was new in town and that she had no place to go. She let him know that she was working up at the local MRO and had just got laid off from work and was only planning to spend the one night in the car unless the police officer happened to know of a local homeless shelter.

He replied to that indication with, "no, nope we don't have anything like that around here in this area." He then went back over to his squad car. By that time, another police car had pulled up as a routine to assist. He handed her a piece of paper letting her know to try the numbers that he had written down but that she would have to do so at day light. He radioed in back at the station to ask if they knew of anything to assist. They had nothing so from there the officer let Journey know that she was not allowed to remain in the spot that she was and that she had to move along.

As the officers left, entrusting her to follow what they had ordered, she noticed that it was pitch black out where they were. She had no idea that it could get so dark. She took a ride over to Houston County to stay in one of the cheap motels that they had over there just for the night.

CHAPTER 10

"HIRED TO WORK AT MRO HOUSTON COUNTY"

Journey made the decision one day to take a drive one day using the back roads of Alabama over to the Houston County MRO.

When she arrived, she immediately spoke with the Human Resources representative that was there. The woman was a super cool lady and she really wanted to see Journey with the job. The Human Resources representative asked Journey did she have a resume. Journey let her know that she did, and she directed her to an online website where she stored her resume and could be located to be printed out for hard copy. In this way, her resume would be in-hand to present to whomever it was that would be doing the hiring.

The HR lady browsed over the resume. She briefly looked over it with Journey to ensure that it was, indeed, the correct version that Journey wanted to present. From there, the rest was history.

The HR lady quickly introduced Journey to the program manager. With Journey's resume in hand, he asked her was she able to do mechanic work? She agreed, "yes". So, he hired her into a direct hire position, and he brought her on as a mechanic negotiating a pay rate of somewhere in the ballpark, fifteen dollars and hour. It was low for Journey but as the old saying goes, something... at that time was, better than nothing. Laugh it all out now.

"Fifteen", Patricia relented. "All those times that you would call me girl, in your moments of frustrations, you mean to tell me that this trip tried to pay you that low girl", Patricia giggled and took a little bit of a sip from her teacup and nibbled a bit on her crumpet. "That part", Journey agreed.

During her work period over to Houston County, Journey made the trip with Ishmael up to see her father on a few occasions. She decided to let him stay with her parents because she found herself in between places to stay while not keeping a permanent form of residency. She took him up for a short while to stay with his grandfather and grandmother for a bit of stability. Now that Ishmael was secure, she took the liberty to head back down to work.

After getting Ishmael situated in the comforting arms of his grandfather, Journey and Tee took a trip together a time or two over to Houston County to go on an excursion together and to have some fun.

There was lots of lip locking. Nails scratching and lip biting going on. He slowly pulled her blouse down her shoulder, and he kissed her down to her mounds. He placed his tongue all over her breasts. Somehow, they both lay down on the bed where he kissed her down to her navel. He worked his way down to his knees and he pulled her panties to the side, and he dug his nose way down into her treasure trove of sweet honey nectar making sure to take every depth of her scent into his nostrils. Her smell made his appetite for love to grow intense.

After a little time, he came up for air. That is when he stuck his pulsating sensation into Journeys cove of nectar. There was lots of pouncing and pounding as their loving momentum grew intense. Pretty soon, the two had lost the bed. All Journey knew is she was lying on the floor, legs up, wrapped around, bouncing from in the air up and down, squirmishing and climaxing her heart out. It was a joi de vivre for her, screawming and yelling in joy and pleasures as his sensation was pounding and pounding her on the floor. She got a pickling. A tickling on both of their fantasies. All life became a blur. All she could hear was her erotic sounds from winning orgasm after orgasm after orgasm. It was a multiple orgasm kind of night. She felt light headedness and she felt demonized from the ecstasy of it all. This was one of those moments that she never wanted to let go of...it felt like paradise.

He eventually let her know that he was married but his wife and himself were going through a separation period. Journey did not fully grasp this concept because she had never been married before nor was, she a fan of the idea. Each time that he would talk on the phone he started to resemble increasingly of someone she knew or had seen before in the movies. He looked like Chris Tucker. "Got it", Journey said, "you look like Chris Tucker" ...Tee smiled and replied, "why do people always tell me that". But before him letting her know that he was married, the two then engaged into some heavy love making.

Tee had his fill of the journey with Journey and his wife began to have tough questions as to where their money was going and about the phone calls and his many disappearances where he was nowhere to be found.

Chapter 11

"APPLYING FOR THAT APARTMENT"

As Journey began to settle into the workplace and to situate herself, she began to buddy up and to meet some of her coworkers. She saw a small few of the other coworkers from the previous job site. She questioned them about it is that they now came to work in Houston County. They let her know that within a week of her being laid off, everybody got laid off. Which made her feel an itsy-bitsy bit better about the nature of the situation, yet still, the memory scarred.

As Journey's days passed by at the MRO, she met a feller named Suga who happened to be on contract in Philly for a couple of years. She and he shared their northern experiences. She had let him know that her oldest child her daughter lived in New York, so to be closer to her she tended to take contracts north yet never really crossing to live in the New York lines. The northern contracts simply make i easier for Journey to visit with her daughter.

One day Journey overheard Suga mentioning going to apply for an apartment. Since he was more familiar with the area, she had decided to tag along with Suga for the journey. **Journey and Suga go to apply for their apartments at the same time at the same office location.**

Upon arrival to the office the door isn't initially open. Suga was already familiar with the property manager because he had visited with her prior to their trip over to see here. He wanted to introduce her to Journey and let her know that they worked together.

They had to wait for the agent to open the door to them. Suga had previously mentioned that he had moved down from Philly after working up there for 2 years. He explained that he had to leave his girl's family up there because things got crazy. Too many people into their business, a thing Journey had not experienced until later in her dating life.

As Journey continued to work the MRO, she began to get involved with a fella named Bubba. He was talking to several women at the MRO little did Journey know. He was also talking to a woman who did not work at the MRO but, this lady was also best friends with the Human Resources lady. The lady's name was Beatrice.

Journey would go on short rides locally with Bubba and all. Not understanding why he was constantly going on these disappearing acts and always had to step away to take a phone call. One day Journey spotted the HR lady out as she was out in a furniture rental center attempting to furnish her house with some furniture. By this time she figured out that her name was Vanessa. Vanessa formally let Journey know at that coincidental meet up that she was gay. That she and her domestic partner were out buying furniture for their place. She took the time to explain to Journey about anal sex, about enemas and other girly related juicy details that entailed too much information. Journey listened. During the sharing Journey let Vanessa know that she was dating Bubba. "Wait, you're dating Bubba", Vanessa caught her words. "Yea. Well, he's a contractor so I don't really take him seriously". Vanessa giggled a bit and she let that go.

Journey one day as she is going home from work, she notices Bubba's truck pulled up in front to HR. She sees him come back out and get in, Beatrice happens to be getting in on the passenger side. She is wearing a very large Alabama styled cowgirl hat. She is an overweight girl and Bubba is super slender. He drives off and later Journey happens to meet up with him at the local bar where everyone goes to have themselves a drink after work. While she is there full of questions for him and tapping him on the shoulder, he is on the phone with his actual girlfriend. He had already separated from Beatrice.

Being that Vanessa and Beatrice were best friends, she already let her know about Journey and Bubba. Beatrice didn't care that Bubba was getting all the girls because she didn't take the relationship seriously with Bubba. She was just having fun. The other women were in the mode of being "the one" or nothing. They were also trying to catch a cheater. Where was "Bounty Hunter D" when we needed him?

While Bubba was on the phone with his actual girlfriend, she could hear a female's voice in the background. She found out who the female was through Bubba's co-workers, and she even managed to get Journey's phone number so that she could call Journey and harass her about talking to her man. Her name was Glenda. Glenda was in town visiting with Bubba in his hotel room for a bit, from the state of Arkansas. She too worked in aviation from time to time, but she had no idea who Journey was, and she wanted to find out for herself.

Glenda took the opportunity to call up Journey's phone with liquor on her voice to ask Journey about her man. He not only was finessing Journey and Beatrice, but he was also finessing another woman at the job. The woman was very beautiful, with blue eyes and dirty blonde hair. She knew about all parties except for Beatrice, and she didn't care. Her name was Sarah. Glenda and Bubba had gotten into another drunken argument, so he had hauled off and didn't return for quite some time. Glenda assumed that he was out with Journey. Journey was just getting off work from her shift and had just gotten into her vehicle.

Glenda insulted Journey the best that she could, but Journey wasn't easily insulted. this is the way that she learned about Glenda, when she reared her ugly head by conversation through the phone. By the end of the conversation, Glenda tried to turn the conversation into her and Glenda alone having a good time together and leaving the man out. Journey was not that type of girl, so she ended the phone conversation right there by simply hanging up and blocking the number.

All the information came out one day at work when Journey was just letting a load off her shoulders at work to Sarah during casual conversation. Then Sarah let her in on the fact that she was with him before any of them ever were. She found out about the others, and she just didn't care. She chose to still mess with him. She let Journey know that he and Glenda were off and on. They were dating for years but they never really stay together.

Conversation ended shortly after, break was over, back to work.

Chapter 12

"JOURNEY & ISHMAEL STAY WITH THE MUSIC PRODUCER & HIS FAMILY"

Journey was distraught. She did not know what to do, she just quit her job at MRO. Everything was getting small to Journey. She took the job as a direct hire, but she had her young son with her. She was not making enough money to make ends meet. Journey had no real plan. She just knew that she needed to go back to contracting because she needed to make enough money to support both herself and her son Ishmael. But she did not have a contract yet.

Journey picked up her son Ishmael from the babysitter Sheree's home and she pulled her car into a grocery store parking lot to sit and think about things. About what would be her next move and everything. As she was lost in frustration and in thought, a family van pulled up next to her to park. It was the music producer – Silas. Silas was heading into the grocers to pick up a few things for the family. He was just finishing his cigarette, when he looked over to the car next to him after taking a puff and saw that it was Journey on the inside of the car. He saw her little man, Ishmael with her. He asked her, "you alright?". Journey stated, "no" and that she had just quit her job and did not know what to do.

The two chatted in the parking lot for a little bit then he invited her to come stay at his place with he and his family. Journey quickly accepted the invitation because what other choice did, she have? She had her four-year-old son with her.

Upon entering his home that Silas had invited them into, she learned that he had twelve children. The oldest became good at playing guitar and stringed instruments. She learned that he did not prefer for his children to attend public schools but to be home schooled, unofficially. She learned that the family preferred natural verses relaxers and hair extensions and etcetera. She learned that the family preferred to practice being Hebrews verses any other religion. It was like living in a little African retreat hidden smack dab in the middle of the country. It was more like tribal village Africa where the natives traded for stones versus a modern-day Africa.

Any time the two went to the studio nothing much happened because Silas preferred to work on his own numbers instead of improving Journey's already compilated tracks of some of her songs not all. The other songs, lyrics were written they were just in need of beats.

When she waisted the day away at Silas' place, Journey grew bored quickly. The final straw was drawn when it reached the family's designated worship day and he made Journey and Ishmael to participate because they were living in his house. As Journey's pockets were empty so she could not escape for anywhere, so she was forced into the saying of 'when in Rome....'

After returning to her designated break area, **she remembered that she had applied for that apartment**. She grabbed her son Ishmael up took him for some Sonic Burgers to keep him entertained and then she headed over to the rental office located directly across the parking lot.

Chapter 13

"JOURNEY REMEMBERS THAT SHE HAD APPLIED FOR AN APARTMENT"

Journey had endured many days of torture before she could remember that she had applied for that apartment. I guess a fit of desperation caused her to act. Journey checked in with the property manager who then let her know that she had one townhouse available. She handed her the keys and let her know that she was welcome to go and look at it. She was gladly obliged.

When Journey pulled into the apartment complex, she saw a tenant that she worked with on her way out of looking around the apartment. He let her know that the apartment used to be rented out by another one of their co-workers and that she had landed a good deal renting the townhome. He asked her when she was supposed to move-in. She let him know, soon.

Journey went back to the rental office and let the lady know that she will take the place.

Journey talks to Silas. "So, Yo Silas", she says, "my son and I are getting out of here my man. We got us and apartment up the road, now what I'm saying. "She let him know. The two of them chopped it up about everything. He is decked out in his most recent Moses outfit, that's what it looks like in Journey's mind. He has a staff in hand again and his Jesus sandals on again. He looks as if he is about to lead the Israelites into the parted red sea.

Journey is sizing him up from the driver's seat in her car, as she had just got into it, as she was heading out.

He switched the conversation over from politicking about life to religion. He let her know that the God that she served was an alien, and that is was an alien space craft that lead the Israelites through the desert. A cloud of smoke by day and a pillar of fire by night. He let her know that this was from the fumes and the fusion of things going on from the engines of the alien space craft. Journey had heard this type of thing before from those who called themselves five percenters, Muslims. Journey shook her head and she drove off, to settle into her apartment.

Within the one-weeks' time, Journey and Ishmael moved in.

Journey worked in the MRO maybe a month or so more learning her skill, acquiring more experience day-by-day before deciding to go back on the road to get more money. Journey had faced it, the money she was getting was not enough to take care of her lifestyle. Journey and her work mates had begun to talk. As there was buzz in the air, a few of them gathered and decided to take a contract out in Okaloosa County, Florida at the local helicopter company there. The drive was only three hours away from Dale County. They had a lot of hours available and were paying contractors very well. Let's go! They spoke.

Chapter 14

"OKALOOSA COUNTY"

When Journey got to the county, Ishmael in the back seat, she had to find herself a babysitter. She saw an ad in craigslist, and she managed to on the first shot, find herself a reliable babysitter. The sitter lived in Okaloosa County at Ft Walton Beach. While Journey's contract position would be held at Crestview, Florida.

Journey sat down in her home. Herself and Ishmael. As she spoke with the woman, her name was Debbie, from the comfort of her couch, she knew that her son would be okay. She realized that she had a grandson close to the age of Ishmael and she had another grandson in his teens trying to find his way in life. The woman also had children around Journey's age. Two daughters and a late older son. He had passed away already.

Through the friendship that she had developed with Journey, she learned that her son often woke her up to let her know when it was time for her to take her medicine. She also had a husband that was very active and helpful around the home. Journey learned the family remained in the home and weathered a hurricane or two that made landfall or passed through the area and that they were not planning on going anywhere from the area any time soon.

Journey worked the place for the first half of the year there, then she quit because she had just dealt with sexual harassment in the workplace from a project manager, one of her upper managers.

Then the wind blew, and she took a job for Huntsville, Alabama. The position and location had quite a bit of unknowns to Journey. She looked at her son Ishmael and recognized that he was not yet school aged so... she spoke with her babysitter from Okaloosa County Debbie, to see if Ishmael could stay with them. Debbie was delighted to take Ishmael in. He even had his own bed in a room that the two boys shared. The other boy being her grandson. They both had their own beds. Just until she could get re-situated again.

Journey worked the military base, contract for approximately one month before getting laid off and having to head back home to her townhome in Dale County, Alabama.

She had in the process been neglecting her car payments on her Grand Am. She had been haggled by the repossession department and just like she treated any other bill collector, she had decided not to take their phone calls.

Chapter 15

"THE CAR REPOSSESSION DEPARTMENT"

As Journey was on her return trip from Huntsville and communicating with everyone via the return drive back, she finally was reluctant enough to take a phone call from the repossession department. She let them know that she would surrender the vehicle to them but that she needed until Monday. The department agreed to Monday being that it was Friday, but they wanted to verify her residential address. They indulged in friendly conversation with Journey, she let them know that she was on her way home currently and would be there soon. She let her guard down because the department agreed to Monday.

As soon as Journey pulled into her place because she happened to be still on the phone with them trying to finish on final details in agreement with them. She was being honest as she could be with them, they were not being honest with her. They immediately had a repossession tow to pull up in her driveway while she was still in conversation.

"I thought you guys were gonna give me till Monday", Journey had said to them. The repossession department were all in the background laughing away into the phone. Journey was devastated. The tow truck driver apologized to her. He saw the devastation in her face as she slowly lowered her arm to hang up the phone. She handed him the keys and he allowed for her to remove her stuff from the vehicle. She was still thrown and in a dismay.

She was in disbelief that they could lie to her and that they were as unprofessional as they were with her and unapologetic. Most of all that they had lied to her face, and then laughed about it like a bunch of school children to her face, over the phone about it.

After the insult and the injury of how the repossession company took hold of Journey's car and laughed about it, she felt that she needed to take a walk and that she needed to treat herself to something. The incident became both a learning experience & a life experience to Journey. She had firmly decided that in the future had she to deal with a company trying to repossess her, an honest woman that she formerly was prior to the incident, that she would be the one to laugh last…

Journey walked over to the local Dairy Queen and that is where she saw him. She never imagined that she would run into him again. There he was again. He had a rag in his hand, he had just wiped down the counters. When she saw him, he was biting his nails and lost in a daydream with a wet towel rag in hand. He blinked a couple of times while in daydream, that is when he momentarily glanced at her. She did not stand out in his mind at the time because as he was lost in his daydream, he just the same kept his mind alert to notices customers walking in. Even if they showed up very briefly just to place an order.

She waved at him, but he did not recognize who she was. She was still scanning the menu to see what she wanted to order. He was still lost in his thoughts, he bowed his head down and started biting his nails, waiting for her to place an order. As her eyes lost contact with the menu, she looked at him again. **This time he had a neutral look on his face, and he grabbed a rag and began to wipe down the counters. She waved at him once again. He still didn't acknowledge her because he didn't recognize her. He stared at her a bit and began to bite his nails again. Then in an instant, he realized who she was.**

"Oh", he said, "I just now realized who you was." He said, "I never expected to see you again…" She thought to herself, 'you thought right' but the way she was feeling at that moment, getting tricked and being repossessed and all she went out on a limb and asked him, "would you like to stop by later?" He said," Yeah", then he acted shocked, surprised, excited, astonished all at the same time. He began to explain and nail biting, "I still don't have no car so Imma have to get a ride or get you to pick me up or…" Uttering under her lips Journey says, "I don't have a car either" she said it looking away from him, pretending that he cannot see her.

"Huh" he stopped biting his nails but hand up mid-air because he intended on going back to it. To biting his nails. Then he dropped his arm, and his look began to drift. He let her know that he could get his cousin to drop him off. Journey began to explain to him where she now lived. He knew the place because he used to live there. He let her know that he got off from his shift late. By about eleven pm so, it would be after that. She agreed that this was okay. He had a smile glistening from his face.

Chapter 16

"BROUGHT DOWN TO YOUR LEVEL: NOW I SEE YOU"

He came over to her house just as he said he would, Khalid had someone to drop him off. Khalid got out of the car, work T-shirt in hand that he was just wearing with nothing but a wife beater and some shorts that fell below his knees supported by a belt, some high-top sneakers, and socks just a smidge higher than the top of his high tops. His bottom part of his legs were super slim yet his calves were larger and powerful leading up to his muscle toned and sculpted rest of his leg. Journey could tell from his walk that he could run fast, the athletic specimen that he was.

He walked on his tippy toes. She began to wonder what the sculpting of his body would look like underneath those shorts, as she was delighted by what she was seeing.

Journey was already in the door dressed in her Fredricks of Hollywood gown and lingerie wear that she had previously purchased online from their store quite some time ago.

Patricia chimed in from sipping her cup, "Girrrl..." "What", Journey exchanged, "I used to be into that sort of thing you know? I used to be a little hot momma, you know that girl.", Journey takes a sip pinky finger up.

There he was. Just as handsome. "You know, if it weren't for the situation, I would have never noticed him", Journey explains. If it were not for the situation Journey would have never noticed him. There he was her saving grace. He finally got what he had wanted after so many months had passed him by, and they both thought that they would never see each other again.

Journey recalled a time that she was driving along, in her mind, while she was in her party mode, that she had an intuitive thought that she was supposed to go to Alabama. She knew intuitively that there she would meet her husband. She knew that she was supposed to had been in the area about two years ago. She delayed her trip and continued to linger around in Kentucky with a very handsome, yet very lost boy.

She remembered when she got into a confrontation with a fellow who brought her somewhere that she didn't know where she was because she had left her car at home, so she had to make a phone call back to the very lost boy to break into her home and get her keys for her. She explained to him the situation of her being left in a place that she didn't know where she was by the culprit, and the lost boy doing so. The lost boy was hesitant about the situation because he let Journey know that he was black breaking into a residence in a what he thought was a white neighborhood. Journey gave him the go ahead and the situation ended up working itself out and Journey simply let the lost boy ride around in her car until she came back. She found out a bit later from the culprit that this was the area that he had brought her to. So she evidently was already in town there before, but she didn't know it.

After spending time with Khalid, she knew that he was the one that her intuition was telling her about. As he entered her door, he held a little conversation with her. He asked her, "why she never called". Journey didn't wanna go into the details of it, that she thought that he didn't value his life and she didn't want to mix herself with someone like that but instead she said, "I don't know". Not wanting to ruin this magic moment. The two began to kiss, because Journey's stress had taken the best of her, and she wanted to waste no time. She felt that they had already lost a considerable amount of time that they could've shared with each other already. She guessed that that just wasn't the time but now was the time. She guided him for the upstairs and that is where the magic happened.

He kissed her all over every inch of her body. The two were caught up in love's spell. The two were body to body, skin to skin and cheek to cheek. Journey liked to stay in close to the touch. Every position that they mated in were close positions. It was night of kama sutra. As the two were intertwined, in the scissor position, he felt all over her body. His hands discovered and followed her mounds of gold causing Journey to moan with just his simple touch. His fingers managed to discover her cove of nectar. He managed to pleasure her while pleasing her from behind her. He loved to be behind her. Him being behind made Journey feel safe, secured. He made her feel protected.

The two stayed close and locked in together as they moved into the doggy position. He started by spanking her and then he pulled her in close to him several times during to deepen her penetration. Journey lifted her knees to wrap her arms around him while he was loving her from behind. She relaxed her head on his shoulders where she could when she wasn't in climax. He grappled every part of her body. From that moment on, he knew that he loved making love with her.

Later, through their time spent together, he would tell her a time or two, "I love fucking you", and submit her with a very passionate, very intimate kiss. He kissed her in such a way that no other man could ever replicate. **It was his signature move for her. His kiss.**

In the morning Journey was washing the dishes to prepare the two breakfasts. Khalid joined Journey downstairs and he engaged in conversation with her. They basically went over the fact of they thought that they would never see each other again. He gave her some inside information of the day that she met him, that he had just gotten out of prison. They conversated a little more but Journey began twisting and turning and everything and moving all about attempting to get everything prepared for them.

Khalid watched Journey intensely and intimately as her attention was divided in what she was doing preparing, washing dishes as well as listening to his story. As he watched her, he knew that he loved her. He knew that he needed her attention undivided. Sometimes he felt that he was geeking on the inside and he never wanted her to know, because it would ruin this perfect moment that he had got himself involved with while interactively listening to her. He felt like he knew her all his life. He was relieved to have this moment with her, he was so humbled and so grateful that he finally got it again. He intended to do nothing else but spend the entire day with her.

At one moment the conversation stopped and Khalid could tell that Journey's mind had wandered off. He came up behind her while she was doing the dishes and he held her from behind. He made sure that he held her close.

"Oh", Journey thought. She paused as she was mid-washing a dish and she thought to herself, I've never felt this type of affection before, from anyone. As Journey was washing the dishes, she was lost deep in her thoughts of making them two the perfect breakfast dish to enjoy. When she felt those warm strong, yet secure hands wrap around her. Little did Journey know, a feeling that she would never get again from anyone else, only Khalid had the ability to do so.

After the very talkative meal, the two shared with each other that they felt like they knew each other from a previous life on another plain. As if they already knew each other and that this wasn't their first-time meeting. They both equally felt as if they knew each other from another lifetime, or on some other playing field.

Images flash through Journey's mind of Khalid in an armored suit on a battlefield, much bigger much stronger but same current build as he was then, holding a battle flag with Journey by his side. He is yelling at her something as a warrior by her side. He yells, "At my command". There is a huge battle raging somewhere on some distant field and Journey is at Khalid's side.

After the meal, the two head back upstairs for another session. Khalid kissed Journey down to the bed. For the duo, in that moment, the love making was more exciting for them both because the two were on a mattress and box that sat low, and on carpeted flooring, so there was no worry about the knocking of headboards.

After their session of love, Journey noticed the tattoos all over Khalid's chest as she lay her head on his chest. She became preoccupied with the inking on his chest as well as the sculpting of his chest muscles and the hairs on his chest. Journey lifted her head as she was playing with the hairs on his chest with her fingers. She didn't initially notice Khalid noticing her admiring his chest. Journey thought to herself, if only he would shave these hairs on his chest. It looks like taco meat on his chest.

Khalid snickered, that's when Journey noticed him noticing her admiring his chest. Khalid enjoyed the tunes that Journey had playing low coming from the radio. The song that just so happened to switch on met the moment. It was a song by the artist Michael Bolton, "Said I Loved You but I Lied"... The tune soothed them both in that moment. Journey rubbed up and down the ridges of his muscular, finely sculpted arm.

Journey then looked up at Khalid and signaled to Khalid for him to wait as she got up from their caressing each other, so that he would not lose that position. She went into her bathroom, and she grabbed a raiser. She came back out and kneeled over him. She intimately began to shave off all the hairs from his caramel complexioned, muscle mounded chest. Khalid watched her lovingly as she did so. He admired what she was doing. As she was shaving him, she would from time to time look up at him for signs of pain. He was staring back at her gently smiling, lost in love.

After Journey carefully shaved all the hair off his chest careful not to cut him with the razor. She took a step back, gave a big sigh of relief and a smile. There, she thought. That looks way better. She pulled back from her position to admire his chest for a bit. The room felt dreamy and livid. She looked back at him, one arm behind his head. Awe, this was such a sexy man, Journey thought to herself. Khalid. Khalid pulled Journey in for a kiss by placing his hand behind Journey's head and bringing her in for the sentiment.

As time passed on throughout their day of cuddling and caressing one another, Khalid realized that he had things to do. He needed to go to the bank. Journey let him know that she wanted to tag along with him. In his heart, he felt like Journey needed a car, so he was hesitant, stuttering and fretting a bit. Letting her know that he didn't at that moment know anyone who could give them a ride and apologizing for he himself not having a car. He began to explain, "my license has been suspended because I had quite a few tickets that I didn't take care of. The day that you saw me driving I was using my mother's car and I was driving on a suspended license. My mother let me use the car to pick up my niece." She let him know that the vehicle wasn't important. That she was prior military, that she could walk. Khalid asked Journey what had happened to her car. "What happened to your car?", he asked. She let him know that she had got repo'd. She also let him know that she had just got hired to Okaloosa County, which was two hours away, but she was unsure of how she was going to get to work. Then he let her know that he had a friend named Dee that lived in Houston County who could give them both a ride to the dealerships locally so that she could look for a vehicle. At that moment he gave his friend Dee a call.

Dee and Khalid were chopping it up on the phone. As they were doing so, Journey began to get dressed. As they were talking, she was feeling the softness of the carpet between her toes and noticing her feet, and then began to put her tennis shoes on for the walk. She didn't exactly know how long the walk would be because up to that point, she had always had a vehicle. Before Khalid got finished conversing with Dee, Dee gave him a later time frame that he would come through and pick the two up for a ride to Houston County – Dothan, Alabama for a car sale from a buy-here pay-here that he knew about.

The two got dressed and began to walk. The walk was long and hot. As they were walking Journey noticed residences with farm animals in their back yards. Like cows, like sheep and goats, although their residences looked like regular apartments. The two just talked about different events and life to kill the time on their walk. He would often let Journey walk ahead of him.

On the walk back, the two walked past a local cemetery. **Journey still walking to the front, Khalid shortly behind. Journey had walked past many cemeteries before but this time she could feel a certain energetic pull towards the cemetery. Journey thought nothing of it. She thought that the energy was pulling at Khalid, but her thoughts were suddenly interrupted by a car whizzing by looking like there as a world-famous rapper riding in the passenger seat. It looked like Ludacris with his big afro hanging out of the vehicle.**

Chapter 17

"THE CO-SIGN FOR AN AUTOMOBILE"

While Khalid and Journey are riding in Dee's car, Journey in the back seat, Khalid asks Journey does she still have her job? Journey mentions that the day that he saw her she had just got laid off her job at the local helicopter company and that she had nowhere to go. Khalid was hanging on to the "oh shit" handle of Dee's vehicle when he looked back at her and he told her, "Well you should have let me know. You could have stayed with me with my mother. My mom doesn't like to see anybody suffer". Oh, Journey thought to herself as she began to look at the sites in the front view window. That's nice to know she thought, had she known then that God was sending her a lifeline.

Journey let Khalid know that she was scheduled to start her job once again in Okaloosa County at helicopter manufacturing company from a town called Crestview. "Oh, then you good", he faced back forward with excitement, "you should be able to get a car." Dee chimed in, "I'm taking you down to a place that I know and from there you should be able to get you into some wheels". "Hope so", Journey's fingers were crossed.

Upon pulling into the blow out sales and pricings on cars, Journey went into the dealership. Khalid walked up to the door with her to briefly escort. He had such a look on his face. He was completely drawn into Journey; little did she notice. Her mind was more of on wanting to ensure that she got the vehicle. Khalid came up to the door of the dealership office to let her know that he would be right back. He had on those shorts with an oversized jersey on., which was baby blue which blended in exceedingly well with his shorts that he had on and the high tops.

Within the dealership the financers got into the details of the deal. They asked Journey for a larger down payment. Which she didn't have. So, the let her know that she could get the vehicle but with a larger down payment or with a co-signer because she was not long enough at a stable address. As she spoke with the financers, the two women went outside to smoke a cigarette. Journey followed them out so that she could intensely think. One of the women asked Journey, "what about the man that you came here with?", she asked, "is he your boyfriend?" This triggered the light bulb in Journey's head, and she wanted to seize the opportunity. She immediately said "yes". They asked him how long he had had residence. She let them know that he lived there for eleven years. The dealer thought, good.

Journey ended up back inside with the ladies and waited for Khalid to return. As he shortly returned, she let him know that she needed to talk to him. She spoke with him saying, "I need for you to co-sign for me". He said, "I can't get any credit". **Journey told him, "I told them that you were my boyfriend". He looked at her with approval and it was so, from that moment on, Khalid became Journey's boyfriend.** "Okay", he told her because he didn't believe that they would allow him. The dealer immediately pulled out a folder with the paperwork. Okay, with your residency and her payments you have yourself a car. Khalid looked at Journey and acknowledged the excitement in her face. He waited outside for her to finish up the process, meanwhile letting Dee know and continuing to chop it up with him.

Journey and Khalid became the owners of a blue '96 Oldsmobile Cutlass. Something that bonded them as it became their new baby.

CHAPTER 18

"THE MEET UP IN HOUSTON COUNTY WITH KHALID'S AFFILIATES"

Khalid rode in the car with Journey giving her careful directions to get to Dee's house. It was late night. Journey lets Khalid know. "You can drive the car anytime, since both of our names are on this car". " I can't drive", Khalid reminds her, "my license is suspended". "Okay, I will drive you anywhere that you need to go because this is both of our car", they agree.

Once at Dee's place, Dee introduces Journey to his wife, Felicia. She is already sipping slow on something, and she lets Journey know that she is cooking some chicken. Khalid lets Journey know that Felicia works over at the chicken plant where he used to work.

As they go more into the night Felicia asks Journey if she wants a drink. She has one, Khalid is already sipping. They go off to play a game of cards. A game of spades. As they are all giggling and laughing and having fun, Felicia is reaching toxic. She continually looks back and forth at Journey and then at Khalid and then back to Journey and she says, **"you two look like brother and sister"**. Journey looks at Khalid, but he is holding in his drink. He could see that as well and so could Journey but they don't entertain what she is saying.

Journey think about how her and Khalid's shoe size are about the same size because she placed her foot into his high tops back at her place and stated, "hey, I can almost fit those." Her feet were approximately one or two inches smaller than Khalid's, as well as in hand size. She recalled how as they were walking along, and he held her hand his hand was maybe one or two sizes bigger than hers. She thought, it's because he is a boy. She thought if the two were the same gender that they would then be the same size. In that moment, she did recall reflecting at him saying that he looks like he could be one of her peoples.

Finally, it came time to leave and to wrap things up. As they were leaving, Dee's wife presented Journey with a big bag of chicken. She said that she had gotten it from work, and she wanted Journey to have it. Khalid chimed in, "you got that from work?" Just then Dee came around the corner, "what are you doing", he said as he grabbed the bag of chicken from her. That was their food, he was thinking and if she gave the food away, what were they going to eat. Plus, he knew that she was drunk.

Journey headed for the car to start the car while Khalid continued to chop it up a little with Dee. Felicia asked Journey, "did they run a train on you?" Journey was taken aback, "what?" "Did they both do you?", she asked, "you know that they like to swing don't you", she mentioned. Journey bobbed her head. She was unaware but thanks Felicia for telling me, she thought to herself.

Felicia spoke as if Journey and Khalid knew each other for a while. That was not so, they had just begun to hang out together due to circumstances and opportunity.

Chapter 19

"KHALID GOES TO WORK, JOURNEY CROSSES STATE LINES TO CHEAT"

Journey gets a phone call from Mitchum, a guy that she had previously met when she was dropping off or picking up Ishmael from Ms. Sheree's home, as she was driving through the small roads of Dale County, Ozark, Alabama area. Journey always loved driving the back roads of Alabama. Most of the time it was very tranquil not very much traffic while traveling. Other times, should you run into a bit of traffic you were stuck behind the soul in front of you. Keep in mind that each driver had their own individual driving schedules on their mind therefore if you got stuck in a one lane for a while until it opened momentarily for a pass you had big decision to make. Either to pass the car usually riding slower than you, which could be dangerous being that you had to ride in the oncoming traffic lane and pray no traffic on came or else that you could maneuver enough should any vehicle oncome or just face the frustration of the ride until there came a change. She also enjoyed the way the sunlight reflected off the trees and the warm southern breeze. Southern back roads had a different feel than a northern or say and out west back road. It felt as if an individual were way down in Dixie.

She answered her Nokia cell phone while driving once she recognized the number going across her caller i.d. "Hello", she says as she answers the phone. "I'm still trying to see what you can do", he said. "You told me that I was messing with the wrong type and that you was the right type, now I won chou tuh show and prove. Whatcha talkin bout witcha mouth. I want chou tuh come through", he said. "Where you live?", she asked. "I told juh I stay in Georgia. I'm in the military over here at Gordon", he reminded. "Ok', Journey said. "Tell me how to get there", Journey said.

Journey pulled over so that she could take down the directions from Mitchum and she was on her way. The road was quiet, and Journey drove fast. If it was one thing that Journey was made for, it was for driving on the road. Regardless of a premonition that she previously had in her earlier days which sometimes made her afraid.

The sun seemed to glisten off the trees, as the sun shined through the beauty of the green leaves on the trees. It had a certain pleasant, calming, relaxing feel riding through the highways of the south. The back roads were the most pleasant. The day was warm, she passed a few down-home markets and a Piggly Wiggly or two.

As she was still riding through the back roads of Alabama, Khalid rang her phone. "Hello", she answered. He could hear that she was driving, "where are you?", he asked. "Oh, I'm just out for a drive", she said. Her phone started to lose reception as she was in conversation with him. His mind got agitated then and he asked her again, "where are you driving to?" He figured in his mind that by now she should be home because nowhere locally took as long to drive. Just then her phone lost reception and the phone hung up on him. Khalid called her phone right back. He asked her again, "where are you?" Journey responded, "huh? What chou say? Krrrrh uh krrrrr...", she pretended to lose reception again. "Uh- uhn!" he said, "I know you cheating. I know you out there cheating! You finna cheat on me?!" he was confronting her. "Huh? What chou say krrrr uh krrrr. I can't... hear you.....", she said lowering her head preparing to hang up, "I'm losing...krrrrrrr...reception..." **"I know you cheating!", he exclaimed.** Journey hung up. Khalid tried to call her back several times to no avail. Journey thought, "I will just talk to him when I get back".

She pulled into one down home market for a bite to eat. Journey swore that the southern hemisphere of Alabama had the best in gas station cooked plates. There were always a variety of assortment of chicken gizzards, or chicken, cheese taquitos rolled southern style, or French fries. Most times Journey could land her lips on a good fried pork chop or make way for a pork chop sandwich. She wasn't a fan of mac n cheese because it had to be cooked a certain way to Journey's liking and not everyone knew how to do that. At times she could even find mashed potatoes and gravy, collard greens. Just some great down-home cooking at one of these southern gas stations.

Depending on if Journey had enough sleep or not, at night, the back roads became a challenge. There was always the threat of dozen off on the road because the roads were not lit well enough when the evening fell into the night. Journey always ran it through her mind time and time again the motto that she learned from her time of service in the military, "safety first". When Journey felt tired, she would pull over and take a nap in some rinky dink gas station or in a spacious side of the road. She opted out of pulling into open country fields like the truck drivers did. Her imagination would run too wild, and she always imagined that she would awaken to some wild animal or some wild half human half something else looking thing that she would have to try to escape from.

As Journey crossed into the Georgia lines the air felt different. It felt cleaner, less allergens. Alabama was filled with pollen at that time of year from all the peanut trees. Although Journey loved peanuts, she was allergic to their pollen. Always made her eyes watery and made her sneezy.

Journey finally arrived over to Mitchum's apartment. She pulled up in front of his place got out and knocked on his door. He answered. He had company over, an older guy but the guy was making his exit as Journey entered the door. When the two got into his bedroom Journey saw a porno hub. There were pornography magazines basically everywhere and pin ups on the wall. Journey wasn't quite sure if she was ready to deal with his type as she wasn't that much into sex anymore as she would have been earlier in her days. Journey was in over her head. Mitch looked at her with intense anticipation. Journey was not even dressed for the occasion. Had she known, what he was really like, she might have been ready. Journey began with a small conversation, not really anticipating what to expect. Mitch quickly grew bored, and he laid back on his bed. He was bored of her already.

He expected for her to come through the door with the fire already ignited. Mitchum pulled out his love handle and told Journey to put it in her mouth. Inside Journey was taken aback because she was not used to a man being so blunt and upfront in the bedroom. She thought to herself, 'well okay' and she knelt down to meet his lust and she put him in her mouth, lips slickened by a mixture of saliva and lip gloss. She went down for as far as she could and came up. "Nuh uhn", he said, as she did not put him all the way in, he told her "Go all the way down". He was a bit long so Journey hoped inside that she wouldn't choke. Being the freak that he was at that moment, that is exactly what he had hope for.

Journey tried again to take him into her mouth all the way until he reached the back of her throat, but she still couldn't take all of him in. This caramel big daddy pop would not go in as much as Journey, tasting his love stick wanted him to he just wouldn't. She accepted the challenge but failed to enthuse. Mostly because she wasn't really into sex anymore.

Mitch became bored with performance, and he grabbed the back of her head gently and he pushed her head up and down on his knob. Journey began to go through a change sexually during to the act. She decided that she did like sex again. She had somebody on her mind during the session, but it just wasn't him. Mitch had opened her up her love. Mitch felt very good to Journey as he screwed the shit out of Journey, which she deeply enjoyed. Punishment after punishment but there was no attachment here. Not even a flame.

Soon after they were done, they agreed to get together again. Journey let him know that she had to get back. When she got in her car and tended to her cell phone, she could see that she had several missed calls. A few from Khalid.

Upon entering her place when she made it home, she gave Khalid a call. "I was just about to call you", he said. "I'm home", she let him know. "Do you want for me to come and get you", she says. "Yea, come on, I'm ready", he says.

Once Journey pulled up in front of his house, his mother was not home, and Khalid had people over. His company did not immediately disperse at her arrival and Khalid said things that pissed Journey off. Khalid let her know, "Yo ass is horny."

Journey loved to fish tail and do donuts, she would just drive crazy when she was angry, especially. From her military drive training she knew what a vehicle could handle and what it could not as she had to drive in tactical situations for training quite often so that is why she would clown with cars. At some times she didn't know her human limitations if anything.

"You know how I drive Khalid. Tell them to move", Journey was at the point of being huffy puffy.

Khalid has a memory of him and her getting into a disagreement while riding in the car. She got pissed at him and swim fish tailed into his yard, landing straight. Khalid said, "Whoaaa!", as if he was enjoying the fish tail moment but he was still feeling indifferent with Journey. He got out of the vehicle as soon as the car stopped, and he slammed the passenger door walking fast up to his front door on his tip toes in his high-top sneakers. He walked on his tip toes because of his athleticism and sports training as Journey would later learn. She could tell that he was very fast.

Later in the night, the two began to cool down their attitudes. Khalid called Journey to come back over, and she did. "Yo ass is horny", he said to her. "I am not", she said. He had a way that he always knew when she was horny before she did. She visited him over his place as he gathered some things to go over Journey's. He explained that he needed to finish cleaning a few things for his mother before they could go. Each time he thought so, he called her out. Each time that he initiated the love making, he seemed to be right. He knew her better than she knew herself. No one would ever match that again, little did she know.

She asked him about his day. He let her know that he just cried all day. He told her about a friend of theirs that he would often drop things off to for his mother because the individual was dying of aids. He explained how sometimes he would just sit at the individual's house and just cry. He explained to her that he would cry a lot.

While Journey was driving and Khalid was riding, music blaring as Journey usually liked it, the song, "Sex with You" by Marques Houston came across the radio. This song sort of became their themed song throughout the life of the relationship. Khalid lit a cigarette and leaned back to listen to the tune coming through the radio.

The two finally ended up over her place and he threw his duffle bag on the floor and the two went upstairs to lay down together and to make love.

As Journey kneel on the bed to admire him, his neatly shaven chest and his tattoos, she was excited about him. She kissed him on his chest although she wanted to kiss him all over. She said, "You kept it shaved", she was excited about it. He said, "yea I did", as he rubbed on his muscular finely sculpted chest. A quality that she would never find in another man little did she know. Journey was once again ready to be a lover girl, thanks to Mitch awakening that little love vixen from inside of her. That little devil lay dormant within her until that visit.

As she knelt on the bed before him, kissing him, he kissed on her slowly and asked if he the guy that she went to cheat on him with was better than him. Journey just continued to kiss him, and she wouldn't answer him, just kiss. Slowly. Caressingly in his lips. As he was putting on his rubber he asked her again," was he better than me?" This time she felt as if tears were going to come to his eyes. Journey was completely oblivious to how hurt that he really was, and she thought in her mind, why does he keep asking questions that he really doesn't want to know the answer to. It was him but Journey was not apted to tell him.

They made love and ended the night with him cuddling her close. He massaged her lower back as he had always done, and he supported her legs with his knees while caressing the back of her kneck with his lips. He whispered in her ear, "I'm going away". "What", she said, and she turned to face him," where will you go?". " I'm going out of state", he said, "to visit relatives". "When will you be leaving?" she asked. "I don't know", he said. "Don't go", she told him, "Stay with me." He had a distant look on his face," I have to. I haven't seen these relatives in a long time."

He held her soo close.

He lied to her; Journey would find out later. He was not going to visit with relatives. He had a drug problem that he kept hidden from her because he was very functioning. Journey did not yet know. He was heading for rehab, and he didn't want for Journey to stop him. He was not ready to expose to her his truth. It was eating him up inside and he didn't want to lose her love or for her to think anything different of him, but he knew that he had a problem and that he really wanted to move out of his mother's house.

Chapter 20

"THE DROP-OFF & LATE-NIGHT PHONE CALL"

Khalid had summoned Journey early in the day letting her know that he would be needing a ride later in the evening around 7pm. She agreed to things just as they had talked about. When she was done putting her home into order, straightening her couches, vacuuming and putting away her dishes that she had previously done before taking a nap in the pleasant breeziness of the day she got out of the house before 7pm to take him to wherever it is that he needed just as they had agreed to. She gave him a ring on his cell phone as he was enroute letting him know that she as on her way. He was pleased. He put the final touches on himself in the mirror like a sweater, a cap and gave whomever it was that he was meeting a call.

When Journey pulled up in their Cutlass he got in on the passenger and he proceeded to give her directions to where he wanted to be dropped. He kept straight across Dale Highway to an apartment complex in the area. Journey was new and unfamiliar with the territory. So, he kissed her and closed the door and she drove off.

As Journey entered the door of her home, she put her car keys down on the end table and she immediately began to unwind and headed for upstairs. She watched bit of television in her room before shutting things off and laying down into her bed. Eventually falling asleep. Around 2 am the phone rang, and Journey picked it up. It was Khalid on the phone wanting to talk with her. He asked her if she was sleep. She said "yeah, I'm sleep". He asked her if she was okay, she said" I'm okay". He said, "okay" and then shortly thereafter they both hung up.

When Journey fell back to sleep shortly thereafter the dream began with the phone ringing again and Journey says the conversation just as it had gone and ended before she fell back asleep except for her dream showed her what was occurring when she hung the phone up. She saw him hanging up the phone and sitting next to the phone worriedly with a key of cocaine wrapped in the brown paper package in his lap.

Journey had her alarm set to pick Khalid up on time just as they had talked about, but he gave her a ring around 6:30a to ensure that she was up. She said sleepily," yeah, I'm up. I'm up". Journey remembered a premonition that she had in a vision while she was awake the week prior while sitting in her hotel room in Oklahoma City. She had passed through very briefly as she had taken a short-lived assignment there in Oklahoma, just shortly before beginning her job in Walton County. This was the reason that she took Ishmael to her father's home up north to Illinois a couple of weeks back. In her vision, which occurred during the daytime, she saw her brother get shot in the back by the police. She thought to herself, if that dream was true then the premonition that she saw a couple of weeks back was also true.

She picked him up at 7:00 an like clockwork just as they had discussed. When he got into the car she asked him, were you doing anything that you were not supposed to be doing. He looked a bit confused and slammed the car door slowly. He looked as if he was hiding something, but no hint was given to Journey through his body language that there was anything that she should be concerned about. "Anything illegal?", she asked him. He said with a weird, confused face., "No" and he began to bite his nails. Journey began to drive and said" oh" and she never thought anything about the entire ordeal, nor did she question him again.

As they were driving along the road to taking him home, Journey was enjoying the tunes that she had playing across the radio. The one that was catching at the moment was Tyra B. "I'm Still in Love". Journey was really crooning to this song as she was caught up in the moment. She was lost into her own world. It was her attempt to stay awake as well as she was missing what she used to do in her free time. She was a recording artist in the studio. She always thought to herself that if she were to ever make it big off into the music business that she wanted Khalid to be there with her right by her side. She always imagined him in her own light, in a white polo and those muscles and a baby boy of theirs on his arms and he, supporting her all the way. She always imagined him in that way. Present. There, right by her side.

Khalid was sitting off to the side, more of leaning onto the passenger side door pulling a drag from the cigarette that he had in his mouth. He was always wondering what Journey was thinking. What was on her mind? He also would always place his hand over hers as she was driving. He was letting her know through his body language, he was signaling to her that he was there. He was in tune to her. Something that she could hardly recognize enough to appreciate in that moment of her life.

As Journey continued to croon to the radio the song playing by Tyra B.," I'm still in Love" the song felt sentimental to the both of them after Khalid hearing the words of it. He gently smacked Journey upside the back of her head as she started to get too into the song adding shoulder motions and the entire bit. Journey quickly snapped out of the trance that she happened to be in as she looked over at him to read him.

He was handsome. Light skinned; she was in love, but she just didn't know it yet.

CHAPTER 21

"CROSSING STATE LINES FOR WORK"

Journey made it over to her gig in Walton County. Her position was a military helicopter manufacturing position. Journey began to settle in well. It was her first week on the job. She was on her way to her hotel that she was staying because she couldn't manage to make it over to her place on that evening in Dale County. She figured that she would drive home the following night. As she was lost in thought her phone rang. It was her friend that she grew up with back in California.

Her friend had relocated to Illionois because she married a sailor who got stationed in the north. Journey and Lala hung out while Journey was in town shortly to drop off Ishmael to her father. Her friend girl's name was Lala. Journey memory recalled the time spent in special occasion with Lala. Drinks all around, pool table time. Even Lala having to defend Journey against some local disrespectful punk talking crazy to Journey and because she was unfamiliar with the way that local carried themselves there because she had been out of town for most of her life and traveled everywhere else in the word, Lala felt she needed to protect her friend just as Journey protected her in their earlier days of growing up back home in California.

Lala shared a story with her while Journey was visiting to her over at her place in the Naval housing unit. When the two drove past a specific home on the route Lala shared, "do you see that house there?", Journey acknowledged using body language. "A female officer was in there with 9-year-old son. Her boyfriend and her got into a domestic dispute. Her boyfriend was harming her and trying to kill her when her 9-year-old son got involved trying to save his mother and her son got killed instead by her boyfriend in their domestic fighting altercation." Journey's face became shocked nearly horrified as Lala were called the details of the situation.

"Hello", Journey answered her phone. "Journey", Lala said, "**girl your brother got shot.**" **Journey grew immediate concern because of her vision earlier on** from weeks ago. She said" Jules". " Ahh" she thought, a small sigh of relief because it wasn't her brother William which she saw in her vision. "Well, what happened", Journey asked Lala.

As Lala described the details of the situation. Everything was happening just way that she saw things in her vision but just with a differing brother's face. It was a cause of wrong time wrong place, shot in the back by the police. Although the brother was really committing a crime the situation was not aimed at that brother. Jules was just in the wrong place at the wrong time.

"Is he still alive", Journey asked. " Yeah, but he's gonna be paralyzed from the waist down", she updated her." Well, I'm glad that he is okay. Lala, girl thanks for calling me and letting me know".

Chapter 22

"KEYS TO MY PLACE"

Journey and Khalid talked on the phone for a while as she was on her way home from Walton County. When she finally reached his home when was not yet ready to go with her. He had the music blaring through the speakers playing that were seated behind the couch. Journey could see the radio and hear the music through the cracked font door with the screen door locked. It took Khalid a minute to hear through the front door. He finally heard Journey at the door and came to let her in. He told Journey to set on the couch because he still needed to take a shower. When he came to the door, he had a towel wrapped around his waist on his perfectly chiseled, where he was notably a couple or inches taller. Journey kept silently acknowledging in her mind that if they were both the same gender, they would be the exact same sizes on everything. Anytime that the two came in to contact with each other they both would say, One or the other first would say," I swear I knew you before", and the other would say, "I know". Like in a past life or something. Journey would have glimpse of a battle. She would always think we could be related, somewhere in her mind at times. She even passed this idea to her father a time or two.

As Journey sat down on the couch, he let Journey know that his mother had cooked some oxtail, "my mother cooked oxtail", he said. He fixed up a nice plate. He had placed smothered oxtail with cabbage, rice and gravy on the plate along with a fork. He brought the plate over to her with a towel wrapped around his waist. He had the perfect chisel shape in this body and the hunkiest walk. The man was sexy. He brought the plate straight up to her and he asked her," here. Hold this for me." Journey gave him the eye along with the plate. As soon as she gripped the plate he walked away and continued to finish getting ready beginning by getting into the shower.

As he was in the shower Journey tried to hold on the plate for him as he had said but the aroma of the meat kept hinting to her nose. She picked up the fork and she took one bite of the meat. Sher thought, he won't notice that. She put the fork down, as his showering was taking a little more time, she thought to herself, oh heck, another rbite can't hurt anything. Then she couldn't help herself, heck this was good. She ate and she ate till shoe found that she accidentally ate half the plate.

He came back out shortly after to check on her but acting as if he were checking on the plate. "Did you eat it?" He spoke. She was leaning to the sided hoping to be given the green light to go ahead and finish the plate. She was guilty as charged." Yes, I did, it was good" she said. He snickered and went back into the room to put his clothes on so that they could get ready to go. He turned everything off. He went to fix himself another plate as he took the plate from Journey to put into the sink as Journey patiently waited on him, but he changed his mind to eat later. He was ready to go with Journey.

It was nighttime when they pulled into Journey's place. Shortly after they arrive there a few boys came for him outside. They wanted Khalid to go with them. Khalid started to geek out, but Journey wasn't understanding him at that time. She was very argumentative and not even playing the game. "But Khalid we just got here and I just got off work. What is happening?", she said very agitatedly yet sternly.

The guys were outside and ready to go, they were all in party mode. One was more outspoken than the other and he was asking Khalid what he wanted to do. Khalid began to act confused and stutter, "well" He was instantly confused because most of the women that Khalid messed with were instantly ready to party, but Journey was much different. She was more of into the quiet nights at home doing nothing but making love if that be what it be. So, he managed to send the guys off. It was completely different than he had planned but that is the way things worked out. The outspoken one said, "man lets go". He muttered under his breath," he act like a bitch!", and the fellers kept it moving.

Once inside the house he noticed Journey's disappointment in him for placing her into that king sod a situation. He didn't let her know that he was planning anything, and she certainly didn't like crowds.

He apologized to her, and they went upstairs and continued into their night. He let her know before going up the stairs while sitting on the couches, that he like to party. He asked her, "you don't party?" She looked at him clueless and empty.

"Listen", she told him, "You don't have to go home if you don't want "she told him. "You could just stay here", she told him as s she handed him the keys to her place. "Alright" he thought. "I don't usually have company over; I am a very private person. I don't really want anyone over to my place. I mean you can have a few friends over is you want to but I don't really like people over", she explained. She left him there as she got into the car and pulled off for work.

Chapter 23

"I REBUKE YOU IN THE NAME OF JESUS"

Journey called Khalid as she usually did on the way home and asked him what he was up to and his whereabouts and things of that nature. He explained to her that he as at home at her house and that he had a couple of friends over, just as she had said that he could, but she was expecting for him to act responsibly.

She thought that she heard someone sniff hard in her background and she was most certain that she heard a female over in the background. "Khalid is that a female that I hear in the background over to my house?" she was shocked and thought that things were unreal. Her mind immediately started to wander but she didn't jump to any solid conclusions yet. Then the male voice started to protrude through the phone in a sound of throat clearing and so on. Journey was certainly getting upset but she had at least an hour and a half left on her trip so she couldn't really do anything. "You brought a female into my house?" she asked him. She ended the phone conversation with him as gracefully as she could and she got off the phone with him and she immediately phoned a friend cause at this rate, she was irate. She called Mitchum.

As Mitch's phone rang," Hello." "I am soo pissed off right now. I want to kill him.", she explained in her angry tone, as she was driving home to get there as fast as she could. "Now what is going on?" he was trying to catch up. "That man that I am dating that I didn't tell you about… I gave him the key to my house, and he has a woman over to my place!" she exclaimed. "Now why did you go and do that?", he asked." I know that they are fucking over at my place. I wanna kill that mother fu---! I want him dead. I want him and those people out of my house. He disrespectin' my shit like that!!", her attitude immediately turned violent.

Mitch tried to calm her down and completely understanding her feelings in the situation as he as a New Yorker that happened to reside down in Georgia because of his service orders to the military." You gotta think rationally, Journey. Don't lose your head in this situation. Just calm down. Everything is gonna be okay. You don't wanna do time on behalf of someone else who out here acting ignorant. You can't let someone else control you."

" I wanna kill that fu--!", she said for one more time. "You know your right...", she thought. "I am glad I called you", she said, "My irrational mind did not know what to do other than to kill and what good would that be if it is to cost me everything. I used to be a soldier myself. I'll call you later", she said. " Okay ", he agreed. He was glad that he managed to calm her down," just calm down and everything is gonna be okay. She spoke with him for about a good thirty minutes of her trip.

He was glad that he could calm her down enough to finally get off the phone with her to tend back to whatever it was that he was doing. As he hung the phone up from her, just as he put the receiver down, he looked over to his friends that were over to his place chilling and sipping slow, and said, "she's going to kill him". They all bust out into a gut busting laugh and started laughing. One of his closer friends says, "You better stand by and wait for that phone call". They all continued into laughing.

Journey had calmed enough to figure what to do next. She said a little prayer. After she sent a lengthy prayer up, barack, throughout the remainder of her drive until she hit the driveway. She thought to herself when I get home, I will anoint my home with some holy oil and pray over my house for all those demons to leave out. If the demons don't leave out, Imma put them out!

Journey started to have vague visions of herself in a past life as she was driving dressed in ninja clothes and held high us on a stake and left for dead. She remembered the first time that she started to have those visions. It was when she was young, and her mother's boyfriend used to watch old ninja movies and those old Chinese movies where the mouth would move something different from what the characters were saying in English. She knew that she used to be an assassin, but it was an assassination attempt that went wrong, and she got caught and that she couldn't save herself from the stake. In that life, she was a man.

She finally made it home and in her calmest demeanor she went through her house to take inventory of what was going on, there. She saw a woman in a high one-piece dress spaghetti strapped with her hair done and her hair down. Her dress was short. She also saw Khalid sitting at the bar stool and facing the kitchen as Journey moved through her place, then into the kitchen area to put her things away. She could also see the male, a tall lanky white guy, who had just come out of the bathroom sniffling at his nose. They all were acting so calm.

Something was going on, and Journey knew it. She thought to herself," what the hell are they all still sitting her for. I am home and I just come home from work. Do they really thing that I want to see their asses in my home after I just come home from work. Do I look like the type that you can just play with? Hmm", she thought, time to go off, it's like a little demon had jumped out of Journey and caused the quiet, calm to move. "Get the fuuck out of my house!!", she exclaimed. Something got a hold to her, "What the fuck are you guys still doing her?! In my house! Get the fuck on!", she said with such anger and rage. Everyone started to scatt, to get going, to move around. Including Khalid and she said to him," Not you! You! Sit!", she said pointing at him as if she wanted to just fuck him up. She slammed her door behind them.

"Are you for real. You gonna disrespect my house?" She grudgingly said to him. She stared at him enough to give him enough time to speak. "You remind me of my mother", he managed to let out very low. She went upstairs and he followed her up the stairs., She was so enraged. She began to pray aloud, and she grabbed some holy oil that she had received in the mail along with her 'bleed the blood of Jesus handkerchief' and she began to go through her house, to try to see with her spiritual sights and senses, what exactly had happened in her home.

She went thought the upstairs areas and she acknowledged that they had been up there but that not much had happened there. She went downstairs and she went into the living room. She moved the coffee table and she acknowledged that the real crime had happened against her there. He could sense and see using her spiritual eyes that a lot had gone on there. She could sense an orgy type of situation had happened there. She saw with her spirit that they had moved the coffee table that she had down that they had just finished sex in her living room when she walked through the door, while she was not present to protect her dwelling place, without her being home.

She told Khalid, **"I rebuke you in the name of Jesus!"** she said, "devil get out of here! Devil you gots to go!"Your're acting just like my mother." He said, "alright, I'm going home. Take me home."

Chapter 24

"JOURNEY & KHALID FIGHT"

Before Journe takes Khalid home, she goes on to change out of her work clothes into her more comfortable clothes. He decides to go into the bathroom and shave his beard and his under arms and his chest and such. As he is doing so Journey is angrily yelling at him for turning her house into a whoe house and for having people over that she was uncomfortable with.

She is also throwing his articles of clothing down the stairs. He is not paying much attention to what she is doing, and she is just letting her rant on and on. Then he lightly begins to defend himself. As he comes out of the bathroom after cleaning out the razor blade, he sees what she is doing. That she is giving his threads a toss. He grabs onto his items from her hands angrily and says," **Girl I aint never hit a woman... butchou gone make me**", then he walked away from her biting his nails. "Take me home", he says. "Nope", she says. " I'm outta here!", he says. "Well good riddance", she says, and he walks out the door.

Journey slowly began to miss Khalid. By the second day in she had given him a call to tell him to please come back. By the third day in she was crying and praying to the Lord for him, the cheater, to come back to her.

Chapter 25

"FLEX RETURNS"

As she was lying on her bed and curled up in a ball, she heard a car pull up outside and she heard a knock at the door and a ringing on the doorbell. It was frantic. She rushed down the stairwell to open the door. When she opened the door, she saw him on the outside and she threw her arms around him. She wouldn't let him go. She smothered him. she closed the door and she continued to hold on to him as he looked at her as if she was something else, "you are something else", he thought to himself. A hot mess. He went into the kitchen, hot and sweaty and helped himself to an ice tray for some cubes of ice and some iced water. She held on to him tightly from behind as he was making himself a cup. From time to time with her grasping on to him, he would look up, as if he was lost in thought.

Each time he was looking towards one of her windows. Her home felt clean, with the cool gentle breeze on the inside. The temperature was pleasant inside her home, far better than the harsh heat and the beating from the sun. Her window decorations were comforting and inviting. Her touch made him forget that he had betrayed her, in her place that she invited him to live in. It was because he couldn't believe that a woman could feel for him. He was so used to being around women who were users and takers. To include his own family of women at times. He looked up because, when she held him that way, he was trying to understand if this was for real or not. Why should she feel like she appears to feel towards him? First the cubes of ice and then over the to the tap for the water. He gulped. She held on to him tightly. Her hands waved over his chest.

She could feel the heat off his body and his heart rate was beating really fast. She tough as she was herself, as she was holding onto him, she thought, 'he must've run really fast to get over here to my place'. By his presence of being there, it made her to forget about how he had just betrayed her a few days ago. Her heart was melting because she felt as if he heard her call and that he held on to every word from her.

She continued to hang on to him from behind. He told her that he wanted to lay down as he lugged his white high tops and shorts, that rode slightly below his knees and skinny legs, desperately across the place for someone to try to sit down and take rest from being over heated as well as with too much poison in his body. Legs a little bit hairy. She had no clue as to his lifestyle. This still was an incomprehensible thing to him in his own right because everyone he knew, except for her, played with their nose. He mentioned that to her a time or two, in their future dealings, in that light to her as well.

She lay in the bed with him. This time holding him so close, the way that he always held her. This time he curled up into a ball and she placed her knees under his legs for support. He stared out of the window. From her bed position, the outdoors had the perfect setting from her second story window. He had a certain stare in his eyes. She held him soo close and she buried her face into his body. She thought to herself that he just needed to calm down. That because his heart was racing so fast that she wanted for his heart to calm down. He said to her, as he was staring out the window," See, **when you hold me like that ...**"

She let him know that she he was scheduled for work that night but that she was calling to cancel and that she would just show up tomorrow. He agreed with her. He said, "I gotta go to my mom's house, I told my mom that I would do stuff for her over there". "Okay", Journey agreed. Wanna just stay over there for the night?"

Chapter 26

"A NIGHT OF CONVERSATIONS SPENT AT KHALID'S MOM'S HOUSE"

He got home and began to clean up a bit. He began to wash clothes and do small tasks that Journey was not detailing. Finally, he ironed his clothes, and he turned the television on for her to watch as he was finishing up on things.

Then he lay down in the bed next to her to watch television. Journey rolled over to lay over top of him halfway as he lit a cigarette to smoke. They were both watching "I'm Gonna Get You Sucka" on television. He began taking drags from the cigarette. The two were lost in casual conversation. Somehow Journey brought up her dream that she had six years prior.

"I dreamed that I died in a car accident. Well, I didn't see the accident in the dream, but I knew that it was an accident. I could see me crossing over to the other side and I saw the emergency lights and I saw my grandfather crossing his arms and smiling at me waiting for me on the other side. There was also a woman with him that I could not at that time make out, she was in silhouette. She had her arms open wide just like Jesus would on the other side, with curly hair. You know the artist singer Aaliyah had curly hair that had the same silhouette when she tilted her head back on that "Rock the Boat" video that she did before she passed away, but these locks were not the same. This woman had on a robe with her arms open-wide, but she was in silhouette, and she wasn't revealed to me who she was. I have not a clue", she shared her dream with him.

Khalid chimed in while pulling a drag from the cigarette and blowing the smoke out, "well I'm gonna die this year". As he shared. He seemed so certain when he said it. Journey rolled over to him, placed her hand to grab his chin and she pulled him in to look him square into the eye as she said, "Don't say that", Journey told him as she was listening to him, "How do you know that? No one can know the exact time of their impending death and be certain about it", she said. He shook his head with his street mannerism, "I know it. I'm gonna die this year", he sat back, and he puffed. Journey simply looked at him in non-belief. He noticed that way that she was looking at him, "I know. I learned this in prison".

A scene flashes where Khalid is having flashbacks of a vision and spirit encounters him while he was lying in his top bunk bed while he was imprisoned. An entity was letting him know about his impending mortality; therefore, he was certain, and he already knew of his death with utmost certainty.

Chapter 27

"THEY MAKE LOVE"

Journey and Khalid make love again going into the night. Before making love the movie still played in the background, I'm Gonna Get You Sucka", on the television as the two indulged into foreplay. The scene happened to come across the line where the actor says, 'brothers walk-in with guns and walk out with jobs. The two giggle a bit at the line because Khalid knew the movie line so well that he was able to say the line along with the actor while he was resting on top of Journey over their foreplay.

Khalid turns the television off because he didn't wanna lose any of the magic in the moment over watching the television. Then they began to pillow talk and he reminded her again that he was planning to go away with family. Journey was not okay with Khalid leaving her, this way. In her mind, he would take away her moment of magic anyway and leave her empty.

Khalid enjoyed loving Journey and he let her know on several occasion at a time. Occasional memories of Khalid stating that play through Journey's mind.

That evening, the two drove around a bit. They went to a couple of different houses that he knew to visit. One of the houses that they stopped by briefly, Journey later learned that he was the dope man, but she didn't know at that time. She had no clue who he was. Khalid went into the back room with the guy while Journey waited briefly in the front room. Khalid let him know that he would be back later. He wanted to take Journey out of that environment and to come back later. He knew that Journey did not mess with drugs neither was it a part of her lifestyle. He decided to come back later without her. "Man, I'll come back later. Journey lets go", he said as they both made for the door.

Chapter 28

"IT'S YOUR BIRTHDAY; I WANNA SHOW YOU WHAT I DO"

Khalid was looking a little worried when Journey saw him earlier in the day. Khalid was screaming for help on the inside but a part of him couldn't let the lifestyle go. He knew that he needed help. So many times, he wanted to let Journey in and tell her what was going on.

Today was Journey's birthday. Khalid decided that it was all or nothing. That he was gonna show her what he does. Either she will accept him, or she won't. Either she was gonna judge him or she wasn't. It was a flip of a coin, and it was all a cry for help. "Journey it's your birthday? Okay. We gonna go out tonight. I'm gonna show you a good time. Imma show you what I do?", he let her know. "Okay", Journey said. "You wanna go somewhere?" he said. "Sure, let's go", Journey was interested. She was all for it because she didn't know exactly what it was that he wanted to do. "Let's go to Dothan. Imma show you one of my hang out spots", he said. "but first I need to go by my cousins spot and get a haircut". "Okay. Let's go", she said.

When they got over to his cousin's barbershop Journey knew who he was because she went to his shop to get her son Ishmael's haircut and edged up. They also had a discussion a time or two about making music and about working to become recording artists. She let him listen to her demo CD. She also came to the shop a time or two and he would be laying down rap for his demo CD when he wasn't cutting hair. He produced his own music. His name was LP.

When the two arrived in Dothan, he was excited. It turned out to be a little hole in the wall club joint with one stripper pole. There were mostly men in the place. Journey and the owner were of the very few females in the spot. Journey had her eye on the stripper pole but no intentions to dance.

Journey had a couple of drinks after Khalid offered her, "you want something to drink?" She had a couple of ladies drinks. Khalid had a drink himself, but he never finished it because he went into the bathroom. Journey went to the bathroom as well, but it was because she wanted to use the bathroom. When she exited the bathroom, she acknowledged that people were being pushy to get into the bathroom, but she thought nothing of it.

Journey sat back outside at the table where herself and Khalid had left their drinks. She looked around briefly for Khalid, but she noticed that he and another feller were exchanging conversation into each other's ears because the club music was soar loud and they were hand shaking. Khalid came back over to Journey, and he said, "Imma show you a good time". Khalid took off again and he left his half-finished drink. Journey caught eye of him a bit but then she let him do whatever it is that he was doing.

The owner of the club came over to Journey, she sat down to talk. She was drunk and she wanted to talk business. "Hello. I'm the owner", she said to Journey once she sat down. "Hi", Journey exchanged with a shorthand wave. "You see that man sitting over there", she pointed out to Journey. It was a man with a ball cap and a jersey, dressed all dark in street clothes. She continued on to say, "that is my security guard. He is an undercover and he won't bother anybody in here as long as they pay me." Journey listened to what the lady was saying but she wasn't catching what was going on. So, she allowed her to continue talking.

She explained, "I saw you and that short light skinned guy go in the bathroom together. Now you have to pay me." Journey's look was confused but she continued to sip on her drink. The owner went on to say, "if one person goes in the bathroom that doesn't mean anything but if I see two people go into the bathroom then somebody owe me money and I saw you and that little light skinned boy go into the bathroom together". Ohh... Journey thought. She means Khalid. Journey corrected her, "No I went into the bathroom by myself. I had to pee". The owner was drunken a bit and was about her money, so Journey had to explain it to her a couple of times before Khalid finally came over. Journey went into Khalid's ear letting him know what was going on. He just shook his head and he put the money on the table for the owner.

He went on to introduce Journey to a man that he dealt with to see if Journey would be interested in a three-some since it was her birthday and he wanted her to have some fun and to have a good time. This was a horrible idea but Journey thought that she would give it a try because it was another man and not another woman.

On the way out of the club Journey handed Khalid the keys to the Cutlass so that he could drive. The streets had very little traffic so she thought, even if he is drunk everything would be alright. Tim, the associate, sat in the back seat. When Khalid got the keys, he started the car with everyone in and he drove the car sideways across all four empty lanes of the road and landed into a parking lot of a hotel. Journey and Tim looked at each other. Khalid said, "maybe we should just get a hotel". Tim chimed in. He mentioned what Journey was already thinking. "Maybe you better drive", he said.

Journey made Khalid to park, and she drove them all the way back to her place in Dale County. Upon arrival into Journey's driveway, Tim and Khalid began to talk. Journey was just along for the ride. The three enjoyed a birthday menage. Khalid and Tim snorted the cocaine and Khalid gave Journey a taste on her tongue. He would not let Journey just do the coke. As it was her first taste, her eyes opened. She immediately felt extra horny, and the party went down then. Khalid feasted on her nectar between her legs while the Tim rubbed on her mounds a lot and tasted them in his mouth.

Tim began first at pouncing Journey because Khalid couldn't get his libido to work. He had snorted too much he later explained to her in conversation. While Tim was going at it with Journey, Khalid could tell that he was not satisfying her. Khalid knew that he was the only one who could satisfy her, and he felt sorry to her because at that moment he couldn't rescue her for her pleasures. Whenever Khalid would touch her, she felt more excited. Khalid's touch was the ticket for her yet, she could sense that Tim wanted to steal her away from Khalid. Was it the thrill of the challenge?

After the session was finished, Journey wrapped herself in her sexy robe and she was finished for the night. She was ready for everyone to part ways or whatever so that she could take a rest. Tim continued to pursue Journey. As Tim had his arm up cornering Journey as if he wanted to stay the night and continue into the night and block out Khalid, Journey thought that he was not a bad looking feller, but she wasn't really feeling his energy like that. She was more into Khalid, who when she glanced over at him, seemed to be insecure.

Khalid walked right up to Journey, after Tim dropped his arm and realized that it was time for him to go, and he looked at her. His look stared into her. His look seemed as if he was silently pleading with her. He felt that he had let her down. Nothing that Journey was holding against him.

As the two were having a staring match, Tim was contacting his people in Dothan for a ride back home. His ride arrived fast. He dapped Khalid out as he was leaving, and he gave Journey and intimate hug, and he continued his way. Khalid continued to stay the night with Journey.

They slowly made love again into the night. Sexing enjoying the night away.

Later into the night as Khalid was side by side with Journey, his arm wrapped around her, both looking upward at the ceiling he told her that he not going to visit with relatives but that he was in fact going away to drug rehab.

Chapter 29

"THE DECISION TO CHANGE"

A couple of days later Journey and Khalid were on the phone together as Journey was driving home to Alabama from the Florida state lines at Walton County. He let her know that he wanted to get married. Journey thought the idea was something to talk about. Then after some time the conversation ended.

Approximately fifteen minutes or so, Journey gets a ring back to her phone. "Hello", she says. She says this greeting for several times because she notices that Khalid had called her back by the caller id. Since he wasn't answering but still talking, she assumes that he must have butt dialed her. She could hear him speaking with none other than Tim from the other night. The two had been talking. About life. He was letting him know that he was tired of the lifestyle and that he wanted to change. That he was tired. That he wanted to get married. That he wanted to settle down. Journey didn't hang up the phone and she continued to ear hustle on their conversation to the best of her ability while driving.

After listening to the conversation for a good twenty minutes, Journey hangs up the call.

When Journey got into town as she began to regularly do she went and picked Khalid up. They spent a little time together. As it was the night before him having to go off to rehab so he had to spend the night at home as his mother Lauren had expected him to do.

While the duo was on the road leading to his home, the two enjoyed the tranquility of using the back road. Tunes blaring through the radio of the Cutlass. **Khalid received a phone call from his probation officer. He let the probation officer know that he was off to rehab and when they asked him how long he would be out he said, "for one year".** Journey candidly looked up over at him from the driver's seat. Her look was in the demeanor of "lieeees", but she didn't say it.

Chapter 30

"TO ESCAMBIA COUNTY FOR REHAB"

Journey came over to see Khalid very early in the morning. She let him know that she did not have to be to work that day and she asked him if she could come along while the family took him to Escambia County.

He agreed and his mother Lauren said that it was okay. Lauren wanted Khalid to have as much emotional support as he needed for what he was about to do, and she also thought that Journey should say her goodbyes because she was secretly not very fond of Journey. Lauren was not very fond of any woman who came near to her son.

Lauren carried along her granddaughter on the Journey to Escambia as company for herself on the drive and to see her uncle off to for rehab. Before reaching the facility the four sat down for a nice buffet style meal because Lauren was hungry, and she wanted to spend a bit of quality time with her son before he would be locked down in rehabilitation for one month minimum. It was the way to make an addict quit cold turkey. Does the method ever work?

Journey spoke to Lauren casually. Khalid eyed Journey as he did not like this. When Lauren and her granddaughter walked away for a bit to fix themselves a plate, Khalid pulled Journey by the arm outside of their presence. Journey looked at him confused and questionably. He said to her in a low voice but sternly, "respect my mutha". Journey pulled her arm back and continued to look at him. Batting her eyes, she felt confused. She felt that she was being respectable. She thought her tone was nice. She thought, she wasn't using cuss words. He said, "you say ma'am and please and thank you". Okay, okay she thought. The meal was a joy and the drive on continued from there, after a pit stop to fill up with gas from there. Which Khalid pumped for her once at the pump.

Upon initial arrival to the facility, Khalid wore a white T-shirt with a wife beater under it, some shorts and high-top tennis shoes, his usual outfit. He stood at parade rest for some reason when the representative came out to talk to him and Lauren. There was a bald guy, a resident, sitting in the front office as well. He stayed to watch the entire intake. In Journey's mind the fellow reminded her of private Powell from the movie "Full Metal Jackets", he was bald and such. Journey loved to stare at people and make them uncomfortable if the need be because once that the jittery energy began to start, then she could then read into them.

Upon looking at this fellow in the front office, once he began to get uncomfortable, one drop of sweat fell from his head. Journey know that something was up with him. She thought something was strange about that man. As the introduction and the intake went on the representative let them know that this fella was the one who handled washing the men's clothes. Journey couldn't help but to uncomfortably stare at him once she noticed the single drop of sweat fall. It brought to her mind the one drop of sweat that fell down the man's bald head when she watched the movie starring Arnold Swartzenneggar titled, "Total Recall".

Chapter 31

"LAUREN TALKS WITH JOURNEY"

Finally, the family van pulls up in front of the driveway to Lauren's house after the three-hour drive back to Dale County from Escambia County. The women arrived back to Laurens's home. Journey's vehicle was parked on the side of the street directly down the lawn so that the family van in the driveway could pull in and out. Lauren pulled the family van into the driveway.

When they got out, Journey let Lauren know, "I work right by where he is. I'm not too far away. Just one hour away. I could stop by to check on Khalid at times." "Leave my son alone", Lauren said as she leaned up against the vehicle. "I want for my son to get better", she said things sternly, "that is the reason that I did this. My son is not responsible. He is not an independent man. You don't want some crack head! I want for my son to get better! Leave him alone." Journey dropped her countenance; she was confused with what Lauren was saying. She didn't reciprocate her feelings. Instead, she felt that he needed more love and more support. She said, "I can't do that", then she walked away to her car to get in and to make way to leave Lauren's house.

Chapter 32

"Journey and Ishmael visit & support Khalid while he goes through rehab"

Journey had since Khalid had been into rehab went up north to Illinois to bring her son Ishmael home. When she went to work at Walton County her babysitter Sheree would keep Ishmael for her.

On early trips to visit Khalid, Journey would pack Ishmael along with for the ride. Usually there would be a family day or there would be a church revival going on.

On one visit, Journey let Khalid know that she thought that the ball-headed man that they met when they first arrived at the rehab, that she thought that he was a gay man. "I mean cause what kind of man enjoys washing men's clothes. Unless he is gay, I'm telling you", she said.

On one visit Journey asked Khalid about his mother as to whether she had been visiting with him or not. He let her know that his mother was paying him visits. That they would talk. Journey would point out things to him that he was doing or enduring that his mother Lauren would not agree with or would make a big deal out of he simply said that "she will be alright". During the same conversation, he let Journey know that he used to play football, and this is the reason that his body was so sculpted. He also let her know that he had had the opportunity to work out while in there.

Also, during the same conversation, he let her know that he didn't really speak to his family that much. He only volunteered this information only because Journey kept insisting a lot that he needed to get closer with his family. He explained to her that when they went on family outings and things that he would go to football practice. He let Journey know that maybe she would be the one to get him closer to his family. "Maybe you will be the one", he said.

On one phone call, he discusses with her that one of the residences couldn't take it and that the first day of getting there the guy reached extreme depression because he felt that he had lost the battle to drugs. The next day, after everyone came back from a group meeting, the found that the kid had hung himself. Khalid said that he felt that he wanted to throw up. Just to walk in on a situation like that, on someone who had given up.

Another time Journey visited with Khalid alone, while she had dropped Ishmael off to the babysitter Sheree so that she could take good care of him while she made the trip. She was having a church revival with Khalid at his church. While she was on her knees praying and really giving herself to the Lord. Khalid loomed over her snickering. She was not drinking the Kool-Aid of what they were selling. Khalid after the service and outside let Journey know that they were just making money and that they did not believe none of what they were preaching.

When Journey would talk over the phone with him asking how he was doing he would make a report letting her know that he thought that the place was a scam and that they were just taking money from the residences there and taking advantage of their situation. That the rehab was all about money.

On one occasion, Journey went over to Lauren's house because Khalid had called her and asked her to go and talk to his mother. he let her know that his mother wanted her to bring him something since her job was only one hour away and she had told Lauren that she would check on him. Lauren gave her some items to bring to Khalid. Of some of the items, she had given her a bag of different designs of ties.

Journey brought the ties to Khalid on a visit. Khalid opened the ties and said that he would distribute them out ther to the facility to the ones who would be needing them. As the two went to deliver the ties, Ishmael seated comfortable in a chair near to her eating on his snacks in the brightness of the Florida sun, different than the Alabama sun on a sunshiny day. One of the ties happened to look extra and fruity. Journey pulled that tie out of the assortment and said, "give this tie to that gentleman that I mentioned to you about. If he wears it, then that means that he is gay. If he declines it, then that means that he isn't gay". After Journey and Ishmael were gone and the visit was over, Khalid did just that. He gave the tie to that man, and he accepted it, with joy.

On another visit Journey leaves Ishmael with Sheree and she goes to visit Khalid. He had already passed his 30 days of no contact with the outside world, and he was finally able to leave campus for a few hours. Journey wanted Khalid to come and see her and spend the night with her on the town. The two manage to land a cheap hotel room.

On the way over gain the room, the two landed at a gas station where the homeless people were there in the parking lot trying to break into a pay phone. Khalid and Journey are looking at this madness and Khalid tells her to back out of there because, "man look at what they are doing. They are literally trying to break into the pay phone. Don't go into there", he voiced his opinion. Journey backed it up and drove off.

Journey recalls memories of a conversation that she had with Lauren his mother after dropping him off to rehab. "Why are you wanting to be with my son? What is there about him? Why, is the sex good", then Lauren snickers it off. Journey memory recalls Lauren getting to the house a time or two while the two were intimate, and Khalid hearing his mother come home and rushing to act as if nothing was happening. Lauren veered at Khalid but presumed to act as if she didn't hear anything.

Lauren did not have the best thoughts about her nor any of the women that Khalid ever dated.

Chapter 33

"IN THE NIGHT JOURNEY DREAMS ABOUT KHALID"

Khalid is happy to finally be spending time with Journey and getting out of the rehab facilities and away from around the lifestyle for a while. Journey and Khalid landed a small room, in the upstairs of the entire hotel complex. A room that was affordable with the budget that Journey had. Khalid had very little money as he was stuck in rehab.

Journey had visited Khalid on many stays before and the two would ride around the town of Pensacola for a few hours, as that was the only amount of time that he was allowed to leave. For a few hours per day on visits.

Some visits he would go with her to wash her clothes. On one of those visits, she envisioned that she would win twenty-five dollars on a scratch off lottery ticket. He didn't believe her, and when she did win after envisioning the amount, he was amazed at her talents.

On this stay, the two stayed in a small cabin styled cabin room. Everything made of wood or bamboo. The room was small, and it was the motel owner's secret. He didn't usually like to rent out that room. He preferred to rent out the larger rooms, the higher priced rooms first, so that he could make his money. On this warm, sunny and breezy day, he could see the struggle and the desperation in the eyes of these two love birds and he wanted to help. He let them in on the secret of that little room, high above with the more affordable price. Sold. Journey and Khalid jumped at that opportunity.

After the two settled into the room, they made love just as they usually did. After their love making, Khalid let her know that he had to go back. "What?", Journey was appalled. "You think that I rented this entire hotel room to stay in it by myself? You better call them and ask for a pass?", she said in despair and frustrated by the news of the situation. Khalid did just that, he gave the director of the program a call and let them know that there had been a miscommunication between himself and his girl. He asked them if they could grace him with more time out, an overnight pass, just this one time without losing his position in the program. The director remembered Journey from the initial visit, and he saw her in his church services a few times. He decided that it was okay, just this once.

Eventually after all the love making Journey fell asleep. She began to dream. Her dream was a very vivid dream. She dreamed that she was in front of two people. They were a blur in her dream, but it was a man and a woman. She had seen these two in her dreams once before. As she dreamed, she imagined that she would have to look for him again because he was not there in her dream. She had somehow lost sight of Khalid. She started to go through a panic in her sleep and she woke up in a panic and a fret. She jumped up, and this time he was right there next to her. He jumped up with her as well, dressed in his white tee.

For the first time, when she dreamed about him, he was right there, by her side. She threw her arms around him to hug. The moment felt timeless. He threw his arms around her as well, simultaneously. Their feelings for each other at that moment were finally mutual.

She was so ecstatic, that this time he was right there beside her. He didn't go anywhere. It seemed like that very moment could last forever. This time, the night had fallen, and the mood was just right. The moon reflected into their room and the feel in the atmosphere of that little hotel room was just perfect. Everything was like a dream. They made love one more time, taking them into the night.

Chapter 34

"JOURNEY & FLEX FALL OUT VIA CELL PHONE"

Journey took on another contract out of state. On several occasions she had asked for Khalid to go with her on contract. He never wanted to go. Instead, he would ask her to get a place around there in Pensacola so that the two could live together.

Journey found it very difficult to do that because the properties had raised the prices on things local there to Pensacola. It was shortly after the Hurricane Catrina had come through the area. She made too much money for the low-income apartments and let's face it, she wasn't very fond of the area anyway.

She instead took a contract or two out of town. She depended on her co-workers at times for help. In her industry they all sort of depended on each other. A thing that Khalid, although he was prior military, never came to understand. Since she worked in a male dominated industry, she found herself at times sharing rooms with her male co-workers until she could get cash money into her hands. Since Khalid spent his time in rehab, he was never available to support Journey on her missions.

Instead, he took to calling Journey out and calling her a cheater and constantly trying to call her to control her. He never really considered her situation. Only his own. Finally, enough was enough and fight broke out. The two of them parted their separate ways. **Journey chose to treat Khalid as if he didn't exist.**

Journey managed to land herself a contract back in Escambia County once again. There, along with the help and teamwork of her co-workers she managed to gain for herself a new vehicle. Journey managed to land herself a Buick Rendezvous from the dealership there in Walton County. Vehicle was fully loaded with awesome.

Chapter 35

"DON'T ACT AS IF YOU DON'T SEE HIM"

Journey and Khalid had not spoken to each other for a tidbit of time. One early morning Journey was home in the cool breeze that swept through her room. The light was just right in cool. In her room she played Kenny G very low, as she was listening to the sounds of Kenny G low.

As the breeze swept through her room where she comfortably lay, she could hear the angels singing a song to her. The angels sent her a dream. She wrote down the words to what they were saying. The angels were telling her through a nice warm gentle song not to pretend as if she didn't see him. She dreamed about the fish market that he worked at by the seaside. She dreamed that she looked all over the place within that place for him and she couldn't find him.

The angels through her dream were tellin her not to act like she doesn't see him because she will look up while looking for him and he will be gone. That he will not there. He would be nowhere to be found. They wanted her to take advantage of the time that the two had been given.

In the words of the dream, the angels were letting her know that she would see him again and that he would always love her. The angels were manipulating the songs and the sounds of the tunes of Kenny G, creating a heavenly atmosphere for Journey to be in, while the spirits were preparing her for the inevitable.

At that time Journey still had no comprehension on what the spirits were guiding her to know. When she awoke, feeling so melancholy and lovely, the spirits were guiding her not to ignore him any longer. To seize the moments. She took that away from the experience. That these were the opportunities with him that she did not want to miss. The angels were letting her know, their kind of love will last forever. The songs that the musical angels were harmonizing into her ear as she slept were sweet, let her know that he would be there to meet her again, on his bed, when she was finished with this life.

Journey didn't understand what was being translated to her. She was just lost in the sensation of the moment. When she awoke, she wrote down the words on a piece of paper, so she could remember what the musical angels were singing to her in her ears while she slept. In the long run, the words, although she couldn't understand them at the time. It made no sense to her. The words became a source of comfort. They were a comforting keepsake for her in the end.

Also, when she awoke, he gave her a call. He wanted to check in on her again. He borrowed a stranger's phone. "Sup" she answered. "Wassup", he said. "I didn't expect to hear from you again", he said.

'You almost thought right', she said in her thoughts, 'if it weren't for the angels'. "Imma come and see you today?", she said. "Huh?", he replied. "Imma come and see you", she let him know again. "Huh? You wanna see me?", he asked again. "Uhn-huh. I should be there around one or two", she specified. "Okay, but Imma be at work at the fish house'. "Bet" she said, "Imma be there".

Journey went into her closet cause she wanted to put on the slinkiest, most unforgettable outfit but that would be presentable enough to wear in public as well. Her drive would be two and a half hours driving from Dale County Alabama to Escambia County Florida in her fully loaded vehicle. Her car was full of gas.

Chapter 36

"SEX BY THE SEASIDE"

When Journey finally showed up, he was quite surprised. He was hauling around a bucket of seafood. Apparently, Jolene, the gal that he was cheating on Journey with was working there that day and she had just gone out back for a smoke. Journey was clueless to the facts but the other co-workers of his were aware.

Khalid scurried out the door with Journey. As he left the towel that was hung over his shoulder he yelled to his boss, "I'm taking my break". Khalid got in the car with Journey. "Where'd you get this?", he asked. "Do you got a new man and he put down the payments for you?", he teased.

Journey turned to look at him and she looked him straight in the eye, "I don't need a man to help me to do anything. I got this vehicle on my own. I didn't even need you to co-sign for me to get the Cutlass. It was just the opportunity we needed for me to be with you. I could've gotten it on my own". She made him to come to an understanding.

Khalid let Journey know, "I only got 15 minutes". I drove all the way down here for two and a half hours only to get fifteen minutes with "you? You are something else", Journey said to him. Journey found a parking spot right next to the harbor.

There happened to be a nice green colored vacation house there. Nice, mowed lawn and a palm tree in the yard. It was off the Highway 98 scenic route. Most of the housing around there off the scenic route were fairly nice. This day there happened to be polo teams in the water that day in their canoes.

Journey wore a form fitting pink shirt that she often wore to the club in her earlier days. The blouse had one strap that pulled over her head. She wore no bra underneath, so her breast were bouncy and free falling. She wore a really short denim skirt with no pantie's underneath.

He sat down under a tree, and he looked so distant. She straddled him and she rode him on top. He was enjoying the moment as he began to grip her and bounce her up and down on him to bring the max intensity to the moment. He came quickly from the pleasure of it all and she held on to him tight when they were finished. She kissed him all over. In the heat of the day, they got up because he had to get back from his break. They sat in the car for a bit, while he enjoyed the view. He still looked distant. A couple of guys came up to watch the polo players from their vehicles. Journey pulled back over to the fish house.

The sun glistened off his eye lashes in a way that she noticed that his eyelashes and eyebrows were blonde. She noticed that his eyes were beautiful brown with the sunlight, like hers, not dark brown. She never noticed before. She told him, "You have beautiful eyes". He looked sort of off into the distance. Lost in memories or thoughts. "Thank you", he said. He asked her to use her phone to call his favorite hangout partners, Tia and Tamera. The husband answered but the wife was gone off somewhere. They asked him how he was doing, and he let them know that he was doing alright. When he hung up from him, he explained to Journey that the duo, Tia and Tamera met each other in college and had been together ever since.

Chapter 37

"JOURNEY VISITS KHALID AT ANOTHER REHAB"

Khalid ends up at another rehab. Eventually, Khalid ended up leaving this rehab facility and ventured to another one because he got tired of their money grubbing. Journey would make visits over to see him at the other facility after she got off shift. She worked the next county over in Walton County. At times Journey wouldn't have enough money to pay for a hotel room and she would sleep out in her car to wait for him. It made her somehow, like a lunatic, feel closer to him. She was out of her mind. Love made her do a lot of the things that she had decided to do for and with Khalid.

One day the guys were out in the yard from the facility, and they were extra mad with Khalid. They said that they though that he left the facility because he hadn't come back in a couple of days so they didn't know how that would go. The guys let her know he was cheating on her. They let her know that while she was out sleeping in her car, some woman would come and pick him up. Journey became infuriated by this newfound information.

After Journey found out from the staff at the alternative rehab setting that Khalid was running off with some other woman, she became instantly mad at him. She no longer wanted anything to do with him. She wanted to cut ties with him before he waisted anymore of her life.

Journey began to drive back home to her place in Alabama. Once that Journey crossed the state lines a state trooper pulled her over and said that he needed to run the car. He asked her for vehicle license and registration. He came back to her car and handed her her items. The trooper pulled her over because he got a ping on her car. He was looking for her co-signer, who was in violation on his probation by not sticking to rehab.

Since Journey was having troubles with Cutlass and she got pulled over by the police. She never guessed it until later in life, but it was more than likely because Khalid had violated his parole by changing rehab facilities.

Journey came to lose the Oldsmobile Cutlass that they shared together because the journeys that Journey took were long distance, it placed far too much of a demand on the condition of the vehicle, and the car needed major repair. She had the car towed when it finally clocked out. Journey had to get a rental car for a small bit. She listed Khalid and Lauren as her contacts for the car.

She realized that she began to think about him too much, where she began to neglect herself. She felt no longer good enough for him.

Journey checked on the condition of the car to see if it were worth trying to save. She learned through this phone call that she had already come to check on the car. Khalid attempted to get the car from under her nose by having his secret girl, Jolene, pretend that she was Journey to get the car.

It came time for Journey to turn the rental car in but she let the rental agency know that she needed a bit more time to turn in the car. The rental car's policy was to report the car stolen once a driver had gone past the allotted rental time. So naturally they would call the contacts listed to find the renter's whereabouts to return the rental.

Lauren went ballistic and called Khalid, making such a stink. Telling him that your girlfriend Journey stole a car and bad mouthing her causing drama between Khalid and Journey. She really wanted to break Khalid and Journey apart. Khalid got on the phone with Journey screaming in her ear to turn that car in. "My mother called me telling me that your stole a car. Is that car stolen or what?", he asked. Journey responded very calmly, "I'm turning it in. I just cannot take time off right now, 'til after work". His conversation was forceful with her letting her know to turn the car.

Journey felt insulted at the whole thing. She felt as though everybody was treating her like she was some sort of a criminal. There was just a big misunderstanding. Journey had poor planning and the car got turned in as she said, when she got out of work.

Khalid kept calling and calling Journey on her cell phone while she was at work. She never answered. On many occasions he would call, and she would never answer. Instead, Journey preoccupied herself with another co-worker who resembled a lot like Carlton from the "Fresh Prince of Bel Air". She and her co-workers would call him, the handsome Prince Carlton, making a pun on the prince from the movie "Shrek" and Carlton from "the Fresh Prince..."

Journey finally found herself starting to miss him. So, one late night while at work she decided to take his call. It began with a hello and greetings, but Journey then let Khalid know that she was tired of his life's drama. His mother always trying to break them up. In which he always said, "she'll be alright".

Khalid shared with Journey, "I am finally paying child support now". Somehow Journey knew that Lauren had put him up to that. Journey said back, "how can you pay child support when you can't even afford to take care of yourself?" Journey understood what he was trying to do but the fit made no sense to her. He was still living in rehab and not in a place of his own. "I thought you would be proud of me", he said. Khalid was taken aback and offended by her words.

As she went back to work on the aircraft after the phone call with Khalid, Journey felt, and overwhelming and immense sense of sadness come over her. She stopped turning the wrench like she was doing, and she dropped her head and she succumbed to the extreme sadness that was in the air. She couldn't comprehend where this feeling was coming from. She did not realize that she was having a premonition. She felt extremely sad for no reason, and she gave in to the feeling of wanting to bawl her eyes out but in the moment, she didn't do it. She succumbed to it. Yet she couldn't place where these emotions were coming from. She was consumed for one good minute with the emotion, and then suddenly the emotion left, and she was back to normal. She didn't know where that had come from out of the blue.

Journey ended up visiting Khalid the extended stay that he was living in as he had taken on a new job, and he had finally left the rehab situations. He treated her to Burger King because that's all he had time for. **While she was visiting on this particular trip he let her know that he used to be in the military. That he used to be in the Navy. He let her know that he had broken his back** because he was leaning out the top of the car, and the way that they stopped caused him to break his back. Journey instantly knew that this was how he was able to pinpoint exactly where her pain was on her back and to massage her back so well. Something that she missed but just managed to do without.

He shared with her that he was working for a construction company. She though oh, okay that'll work.

It was mid-month in October when Khalid just came up missing. Journey looked for him for approximately a week. She phoned his mother Lauren to see if she had heard anything. Lauren hadn't heard anything. She expressed her fear to Lauren since he was working at a construction site that since no one had heard from him that he could turn up dead. With his lifestyle and the whole bit.

A week later he called Journey and let her know that he was in jail. He was in jail from what sounded like dealer charges. Resin on his hands, resin on his feet, resin on his cell phone but nothing in his system.

While in the extended stay with him after their making love. His body impeccably sculpted as usual, his phone rings when he goes away to get them refreshments from the vending machine. His phone rang alot when the two of them were together but Journey thought nothing of the buzzing. He was a free man now, free from the grips of rehab. While he was away, she catches a glimpse of the picture coming across the screen with the number, a female. She catches the name Jolene. She sees that she is pretty.

Khalid walks back in just in time to see Journey looking at his phone. "Who is that?", Journey asks. " My new girlfriend", he says. "She is pretty", Journey compliments him. "Thank you", he said. "Do you love her", Journey asks him. "Yes but...", he holds himself from saying.

Journey already knows what he wanted to say. "Yes, but not like you", because after that. He hesitated to say on quite a few occasions. He missed his mark every time. He always wanted to say, "not like you and "she isn't you" but the two never could get their feelings together enough for each other to just be, together.

Ever since that premonition, things became, bittersweet between them. Love unrequited.

Chapter 38

"Journey tells Khalid 'Bye' "

Journey runs a summary in her head of all the bull crap that she had taken off Khalid. She gets off the phone with her cousin, Marla, letting her know that she is on her way up to Kentucky because she needed a place to lay her head once again, for a while.

As she gets off the phone with her cousin, she gets a call from Khalid. "Are you okay?", he asks. "Yeah, I'm okay", she responded. Khalid could feel that something was gonna happen. He recalled their late-night conversations at his bed at his mother's house. A part of him wished that things could go back to the way they were between himself and her before he had made the decision to leave town. Yet a part of him didn't want to return to that. He was in trouble with the law.

Then she went on to say, "your girlfriend is pretty". "Yeah but...", as he wanted to say for so many times, but he never worked up the way to know how, she's not you. He wanted to say but he never took the chance to say.

Then suddenly Journey feels free to say, "I can't take this no more, so I'm leaving. I thought that it was me and you, but I see that you have moved on. I never really thought this would happen. So, I'm leaving. Bye Khalid", she told him.

Then the two hung up.

Chapter 39

"JOURNEY GOES TO BE WITH HER COUSIN IN CLARKSVILLE, KENTUCKY"

He had called for her at her cousins before. Memories flash through Journey's mind as she drives cross country. Memories of her staying with her cousin struggling as he just remained in rehab oblivious to anything going on in the real world. When the struggle was too real. This time though things would be different. Journey was done for the most part and she had told him 'Bye'.

Journey crossed Kentucky state lines and finally Journey had reached to her cousin Marla's home. Marla peeked out the door from the upstairs rear apartment of her apartment unit to see Journey in a white vehicle.

Journey reached to her top apartment. "How you doing gal?", Journey talked with her cousin. "I'm glad you made it cuz", she hugged her cousin Journey so close. "Okay", Journey thought in her head. "I bought a new car', Journey said with excitement. Her cousin dropped her shoulders and went into the house and took a puff of her smoke, "I see that". Journey said, "Let's go out tonight", Journey had said. She just wanted to unwind from the stress of the road and from leaving her old world behind, so she thought, at that moment in time. "Just like old times", her cousin said. "Just like old times", Journey confirmed. "Let's go out unwind and have some fun." "Okay", her cousin said.

The girls were doing their hair. "Girl you gotta check out that car", Journey began, "I got the heated seats". "Oh yeah. Let's go check it out", Marla said. Marla was not very impressed with the car, but she was very impressed with the heated seats.

Journey made a run to the nearest labor pool to try to figure out if she wanted to work the joint to have the opportunity to find some money so that she could have money to take off from her cousin's place if she needed to. As you know, Journey was always on the go and she needed funding to take flight with. While she was out and about in her temp agency search, she received a phone call from a headhunter that she was familiar with. They asked her if she was interested in a leadership position, based on her resume she seemed like a good fit. Journey agreed. All she could do was try. The recruiter asked Journey to hold the line, they wanted to give her an on-the-spot interview with the hiring manager for a startup business jet company out of New Jersey. Via telephone, everything sounded copasetic, everything checked out good.

The girls went out, had a good time. Then Journey got a call from a headhunter letting her know that she got accepted for a job out in New Jersey. She interviewed a little over the phone and she decided that she would come up for the position.

Later into the night Journey and Marla were in deep conversation when Marla said, "I had a dream about you. I saw you die in a car accident. This accident was really bad. It was a white car involved in the accident." "What?", Journey said. Confused. A bit on edge. She could feel hairs raise on her arms, but she was not sure if she should be scared because it was…just a dream. From the look on Journey's face, her cousin felt that she needed to make her believe her. "How do you think I know that you were gonna pull up in a white car when I peeped out? I thought, 'oh no, she's in the white car'… instantly my heart dropped. In my dream you died". Her cousin Marla began to cry at this time, and she got real emotional. Journey realized that her cousin had had a premonition. She told her, "God is in control cousin. If I die, then it was just my time. Barack. Let's send our prayer's up."

A couple of days later, Journey left for New Jersey.

Chapter 40

"KHALID'S DEATH"

Khalid was going through the struggle that day, as the two had usually went through on any other day.

He was on the phone with his mother Lauren for the longest. Prior to that, Jolene. He was on the phone in the back of the restaurant for a couple of hours in a heated argument with someone. Little did anyone know; it would be his last meal. He had a nice plate and a couple of beers. He didn't have the money to pay for his meal. The restaurant owners really began to press him for his tab. He tried to skip out on his meal as he did now newly reside with his boss from the construction company so, he happened to live close to the place in the neighborhood. So, he thought that he could escape.

The restaurant was fenced in with a really high wooden gate. As athletic as Khalid was at his tab skip out on his meal, he jumped the restaurant's fence, and ran smack dab into traffic. It was holiday time. There happened to be a white truck with a 19-year-old driving the truck. He was turning the corner fast in the late evening, turnin the corner at 30-mph, is the story that Journey gathered from the newspaper about an Alabama man.

Journey's Alabama man trying to lead a Florida life.

"Oh my God", when **Journey found out two-weeks later** by attempting to visit him in his establishment at his boss' place. She had just come back into town, with a lot less money than she planned on having. She wanted to ask him for a loan. She expected to ring his doorbell and they argue for a bit, and then he would give her the money because he would always do for her.

Instead, she was met by his boss and his boss' wife holding back tears, handing her Khalid's obituary. Letting her now that they had just come from his funeral service in Alabama.

In hindsight twenty-twenty Journey found out through reading the Escambia County newspaper and through talking to the people who were present when it happened, and from her own premonitions and her cousin Marla's premonitions and from talking with Lauren, Journey learned and pieced together the details of the accident.

Chapter 41

"WHILE BEING IN NEW JERSEY"

Journey had reached her hotel room at the township in New Jersey where she would be working. She unpacked her travel bags from her car, on her first night in township, and she went upstairs to her room to settle herself in to her room, as she always did on a trip. She took a rest and then she showed up for work the following day.

Upon her arrival to her job, she quickly began to realize that she did not fit in to the position very well as was previously discussed during interview over the phone. The hiring manager spoke with her a little further while he had her there in person. She felt overwhelmed inside but tried her best not to let it show. The manager let her know that they were looking for someone more of for a supervisor position. Journey felt inside, no, that she didn't fit in with that.

Journey went back to her hotel room that day and she went to the gym for her usual routine of working out. She went running on the treadmill that evening as she would usually do, since leaving the military. As she got up to a certain speed, Journey noticed that her focus had to change so that she could maintain her body rhythm and everything else. Journey, since her brain had switched waves, she could sense that someone was looking at her throughout all the many mirrors that that gym had.

Suddenly as she was beating foot on the treadmill, she saw a black streak swerve out to in front of her. She could make certain things out clearly. She saw the figure look down at her feet, look up at her face, acknowledged that she saw its face. The figure had a shocking look on its face as if to say "she saw me" and then it whisked off.

Journey saw the figure. She saw the reactions on the face of the figure. She thought nothing of it because she remembered her mother telling her that she was going into the mountains with other Buddhists, as Journey had a memory recall of the telephone call. She thought it was her mother and didn't make much of a big deal of it. She knows how Buddhists can control their energy, their chi and their body temperatures. They could move out of body if the need be. After all her mother did say that she was going into the mountains with her monastery. The figure reminded her of a Tom & Jerry cartoon, when the duo was messing around and harassing each other, and they would whisk off. Or Roadrunner, or Speedy Gonzales or anything that was fast.

She went to her hotel room, and she had a night out on her second night in township. She met a guy, and they later went back to her hotel room and had a round of casual sex. As she was being pleasured by the guy, she started to have memories of Khalid. She thought, that, this one was not as good as Khalid. As they continued into their pleasure, Journey could feel that someone was looking at her from the corner of the hotel room. The feeling was strong but nothing she continued to wonder about.

Her third day in town she met with the hiring manager. He let her know that he had to let her go because she was not what they were looking for, but they wanted her to be able to stay a few days so that she could make herself some money, instead of getting turned around.

Journey in her disappointment at the entire situation went to her hotel room to make a phone call to let her headhunter agency know what was going on. **As she sat on the hotel bed to dial them and eventually the phone began to ring on their end, Journey felt the bed lean down as if someone had sat beside her on the bed,** she looked to the side of her while holding the phone. When she looked down at the bed, **she saw butt cheek prints as if someone who was not visible to her eye, had sat down there beside her.** Journey lifted one leg. She was about to hang up the phone and call to the front desk and ask them if anyone had passed away in that room before in a stay, but she didn't. Journey just held on to the mystery of it all.

Journey had gotten an advance on the three days from her agency and was considering heading back onto the road. She wanted to go back to see him. She wanted to see Khalid. She began to miss him again. She knew what she needed. She needed Khalid, but she needed to work up her nerves first so, she thought that she would take her time on the road because she had a long drive, and she didn't want the anxiety of the moment. She was hoping to be able to patch things up with him.

Journey recalled that the last time that she had talked to him, she had fish tailed out of a gas station not too far from where he was staying, at the room-for-rent and left him high tale, athletic walking. He let her know that he had moved on with Jolene. A girl from Turkey. She recalled that she asked him if he loved her, and he said yes but not like you. She recalled that their argument was heated. She was bent on getting her lover back. She recalled driving across that bridge and being on the cell phone with him when she told him 'Bye'. She thought to herself, I should've never told him by.

Journey had packed all her things into her car. Journey was a movie watcher, as she was. She loved a good motion picture film. She decided to stop off to the local movie theater before she got on the road as she at times would do. As she was heading to the big screen, she passed a neon lit building that was psychic, palm reader building. As she looked at the neon lighting of the place, she felt a big pull to stop over there. She didn't really want to hear what madam says a lot had to say so she drove past it the first time.

As she was heading for the big screen, she realized that she wasn't really in the mood to watch a movie after all. As she was leaving the parking lot of the cinema, she saw the neon lights of the psychic house again. This time she felt a huge urge to pull into the driveway there. So, she did. She thought, oh what can it hurt, I'll just see what the madame must show me. If she even says to me anything at all.

Once inside, the psychics voice sounded like a man, rather masculine. She told her to sit down. She was rather interested in speaking with Journey. As she sat Journey down on the couch, she said that she needed to do a full reading on Journey.

"Okay" Journey said. Whatever that is, she said. "How much that cost?", Journey asked. "$50", the psychic woman said. Journey pulled out a crispy $50 dollar bill USD. The woman was stirring her tea that she had in her hand, and she leaned into the cards, and she said, "I see that you have a lot of money and that you work like a man", she said, "you look like a woman, yet you work like a man". She said, "I see that you have lived many lives". Journey said, "really. What life am I on now?" The woman sipped from her cup, and she stirred into her cup a little bit more and she said," seven. You are on life number seven now". She leaned into the cards once again and she looked to be in shock as she said, "I see an accident. It's a tragedy".

Journey immediately took over, "I know because I keep feeling this weird energy around and I saw myself die in my dream that I had a long time ago but...", she began shaking her hands from nervous energy, "and my cousin told me that she had a dream that I died in a car accident, and I've always been told be careful how I drive". The woman looked in at the cards again and she said, "I see an evil spirit around you. How do you know that this didn't happen already?" "What?", Journey then began to get confused. "That energy, that's him. That's the guy. The love of your life?? You two never made it because you must dream of each other when you both lay down at night. He says that he loves you dearly." "Who?", Journey said. She had not a clue.

"Well, I am going back home", Journey let her know. "How much money do you have?", she asked Journey. "Give me $150...", she hung her hand out, "all of it. Give me all of the money that you have".

Journey did not respond to her asking. She was still in dismay about the accident. Journey had not a clue. Who was she talking about? The woman was trying to stop Journey from going down south. She wanted to slow down her trip, bring it to a halt, as well as make a little money off her tragic information.

"I see that you make a lot of money", she said. "I'm gonna need $75 to keep talking", she said. "$75?", Journey replied. "Hey", she said, "I'm giving you information here, you're paying me for information", she informed Journey. "Okay", but I have to go to the ATM to get it". "Okay", the woman said, "and bring back a pair of pants".

Journey went on her way; she went to the nearest Target. As she was searching for the item and planning to get cash back at the register, she picks up the phone to dial Tom. Now Tom was a guy that she dated on and off while Ishmael was young. She still resided near a military community in Tennessee, and she thought he was the one that the woman was speaking of. She called Tom, when she stopped at a clothing rack. She was reluctant that he answered the phone. She spoke with him for a bit and then she blurted out the words, "I love you" to him. He responded, she had said that to him before in her early days of spending time with Tom, when she really felt hooked to Tom.

She could feel someone peering back at her from the other side of the clothing rack, but she saw no one. She felt nothing those, words of 'i love you' rolled off her lips to Tom. She suddenly could feel someone looking deep into her. She knew that Tom wasn't the one that the psychic woman was talking about. She cut the phone conversation short.

She made it back to the psychic woman's establishment. She dropped the pants off and she didn't stay. The woman told her to be careful.

Journey was confused and scatter brained the rest of the way. She couldn't figure things out.

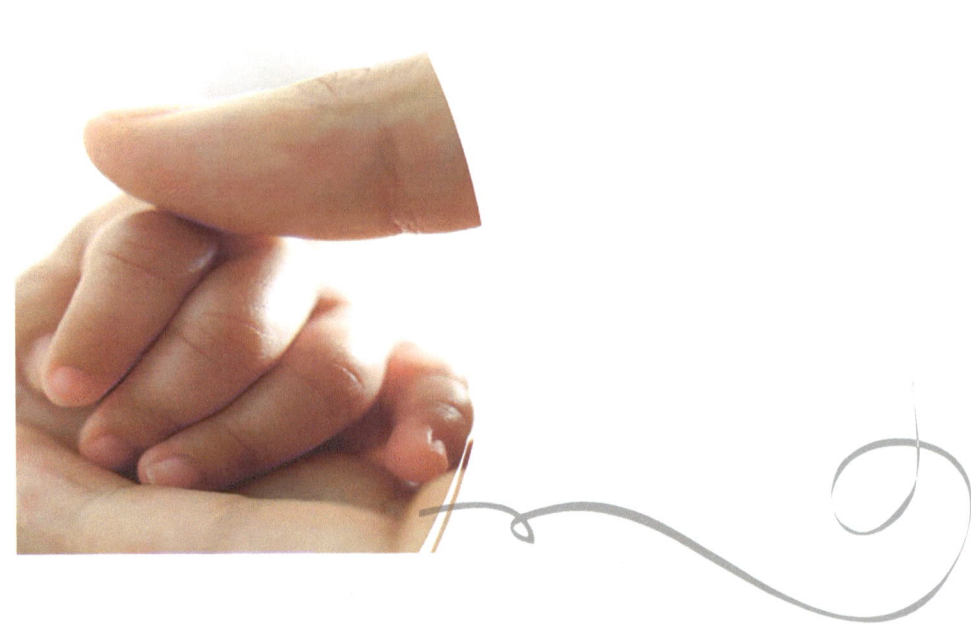

Chapter 42

"I MISS YOU"

Journey had already had her son, Khalid. Khalid did not belong to Khalid, no. Journey just jumped on the first man that she saw in her desperate attempt to wipe clean all memory of Khalid.

She remembered the nights that the late Khalid and herself had stayed up talking about having a baby together and the possibility of starting a family. These things never had the chance to come about because he lost sight of their discussions seemingly as well as the unfortunate tragic turn of events that altered the course of Journey's life forever.

She remembered her dreams of him when she immediately went on assignment taking her son Ishmael with her again. She remembers that one night straight for a week, Khalid would come into her livid dreams and make love to her. Her dreams stop by the end of that week once that her conscious mind took over.

She had visited his grave site a time or two in the past, but she realized that he was not there. She was disappointed that his libido had now become meat for worms. 'How could his love be down there when he was supposed to be here with me' was one of her thoughts she had when she got lost. She left picture memories of the the two together a time or two on his grave. They really loved each other over that short summer.

A little over a year had passed. Over the entire year of his passing, he liked to leave Journey suttle hints that he was still around. His mother Lauren's home smelled a certain way, which Journey learned years later that the smell was dry cleaning. That smell would come in immensely strong every day for the entire year on the first year of his passing. They really loved each other. It's too bad that they both didn't know it until it was too late. Unrequited love.

When Journey would lay at night with her two boys, Khalid as little as he was and Ishmael, nearby. She would often fantasize that Khalid was laying right behind her where she lay, on her bean bag set up and with pillows, on the floor near the baby. She had a picture frame of him that she found, because she remembered that she had taken pictures of him in her camera that was not developed prior to his death. When she found those pictures in her developed photos from Walgreens, she cherished the photos. She at times would sleep with the picture in framed. Like he was still alive. Eventually she hung the picture up on the wall of her place.

Khalid's birth was not an easy one. He had to stay in the hospital for a week after his birth because he managed to swallow some of the amniotic fluid. The late Khalid gave the little guy a piece of his essence at his birth to sustain the feller.

As she lay on the floor setup, she had her radio playing as she would usually do, listening to the tunes of Brian McKnight, "I Miss U", when his voice came across the radio saying, "I Miss You" in the words of the song. She heard the late Khalid clearly. She missed him and she loved him even more.

Chapter 43

"I WILL ALWAYS LOVE YOU"

Journey turned to her son Khalid, "I loved him so much my son, that I named you after him. He was my late friend, and I loved him. I had never been able to be loved the same since him, but I managed. I gave you his name so that I would never forget him, no matter how hard I might try to."

Khalid asked, "Is that why his mother Lauren did that to me?" "More than likely son", she said, "but that we will discuss a little later. That woman was in misery… and misery loves company. When she marched your brother and yourself over to Department of Human Resources Child Protective Custody, it was the anniversary of the anniversary of her son's death, my late friend. This woman was in misery. She was miserable, she acted greedily and miserably against us. I had many challenges over our separation to see God's hand in this entire process at separation my son."

Khalid questions his mother with intent. "Did you ever momma?" "For such a time as this", she said while she was lost in thought. "You know, he came to me a long time ago in a dream", flashes of the dream run through Journey's head. "He apologized to me. This was maybe a week or two before you were conceived", she looked at Khalid and then looked away she went back into thought from it, "he told me that there was going to be an accident. At that time, we were in Amish town, and they all drove horse and buggies. There was heavy penalty to pay should someone run into one of those things. You were better off hitting a car than one of those Amish man horses", she said with intent.

"Oh really! An accident momma", he digressed. "Now baby you were no accident. What I was saying was I was still so alert to my own demise at that time, and he had just had his demise that I was literally looking for an accident. Nooo, he was talking about yo daddy...he was an accident. **You would've been my friend's baby, loved and cared for with the utmost care with Khalid as your father, instead of your father but you baby... you were no accident! You're my life!**", she deeply hugs Khalid and kisses him on the forehead.

About the Author

Juleane Sawyers, I reside in Miami, Florida. I was raised in Long Beach, California. Throughout my high school years I discovered my love for writing. It was my way to escape. I learned to proofread, write, and edit at a very early age. As a matter of fact, I was very fond of it. I went to theatre classes and I learned to write stage plays and screen wrights. I moved a lot, so I lost many manuscripts along the way. I have previously tried to write this one yeaFs ago but I was unsuccessful at completing it until now, I had firmly decided to take that chance and to write. After my significant other constantly telling me that I need to become a story writer. He had jokes but I decided to take it seriously as a past time, post pandemic with the possibility of more commotions concerning pandemics coming up in the future. This is the world that we have now come to live in. In high school years, my stories were generally energetic and exciting, allowing the reader to escape into the moment of the story telling.

Milton Keynes UK
Ingram Content Group UK Ltd.
UKHW051826110224
437601UK00002B/45